R - BNE 8/3

UNFINISHED BUSINESS

Unfinished Business

A NOVEL OF SOUTH AFRICA

by SHEILA GORDON

CROWN PUBLISHERS, INC., NEW YORK

Library of Congress Cataloging in Publication Data
Gordon, Sheila.
    Unfinished business.

    I. Title.
PZ4.G666Un   [PS3557.0687]   813'.5'4   74-30395
ISBN 0-517-51905-4

PART ONE

I

Father is dying, so they are allowing me to come home. They are allowing me to come home for one week.

One week.

The plane moving steadily through the black night, in a straight line, from London to Munich, then south, over the Mediterranean and down the vast length of the African continent.

Ten years. Ten years since I have smelled the sharp dry air of Africa. Ten years since I have been dazzled by the cutting brilliance of the African sunlight. Ten years since my skin has been touched by the steady burning heat of the African sun.

London this evening. Clenched in the fist of the February chill. The damp that enters the marrow so that it is hardly possible to remember how it felt to be warm. At the airport, Margot, with the children huddled desolate about her in the drizzling rain. The two older ones remembering perhaps the dislocation, the jolt of disbelief at the time of the arrest when their small world was tossed into the unfamiliarity of chaos. Of nothing to be taken for granted again. Nothing to be assumed. Ordinariness, routine, dailiness, all suspect. The knowledge of the abyss that skirts the familiar road.

Drinking tea, too strong, too sweet, at the airport cafeteria, Margot's eyes and the London dusk dark with apprehension, intimations of fearfulness. The children silent in the face of the double menace of death and imminent separation. Father's dying overshadowing all the other phantoms that they thought had been exorcized by the sanity, the rationality, of ten years in London. Both of them conscious every moment, in the commotion around them, of the gentle old man dying, alone, in the house in Johannesburg.

Margot, drinking her tea, the cup clasped in both hands. Behind her dark eyes he knew what memories were stirring. His arrest. His disappearance. His utter inaccessibility. Her flight with the children. The uncertainty of ever seeing each other again. The betrayals. Worse, the fear of betrayal, as corrosive, debilitating as the reality.

Margot's pale skin startling the recollection of the dark honey of Zainab's complexion, the scent of syringa, the surgical swiftness of their separation. The sediment that had drifted down, settled at the bottom of the ten years, being stirred up again, surfacing.

Sipping the sweet strong tea at London airport, his wife and children grouped around him at a chrome and plastic table, he felt helpless in the grip of his wretchedness. It pressed down on his brain, his chest, his stomach. Outside, in the gloom of dusk, the rain wept softly down on the huge plate glass windows. His existence seemed bounded by death, disappointment, and a vast pointlessness.

The youngest child, the one who was born in London, said, "Lucky Dad, you're going to the middle of summer."

He thought of his father dying in the middle of the glorious highveld summer.

The smooth emotionless tones of a computerized girl

announced his flight departure. They abandoned their table with its litter of empty cups, crumpled paper napkins, and spilled sugar, and moved to the exit barrier. He kissed his three sons. The cheek of the oldest bristling with fine gold. The boy was discomfited, the situation, so charged with memory of fear and loss, and now overlaid with knowledge of death, too much for the naturally chaotic condition of a seventeen-year-old to encompass. The middle boy, with Margot's dark solemn eyes, hugged him tightly, angrily brushed tears from his smooth cheek. The youngest, the Englishman with the Limey accent, the only native in the family, the only nonexile, the one without memories, covered his face with kisses, begged him not to forget to bring back an ostrich egg.

Margot. He and Margot looked wordlessly at each other. The flight was called again. Panic lunged. He kissed her peremptorily. He said, "It will only be a week." At the turnstile he showed his documents to the official at the desk, turned around and saw them, his family, huddled together beyond the barrier. A vast pity for himself and them rose up, distended his throat. He waved, turned, and strode off through the crowded lounges, down the hollow impersonal corridors, out onto the gloomy tarmac, and mounted the steps of his plane.

2

The heavy gutturality of the accent of the middle-aged Afrikaans woman in the seat beside him started up the fear again. Her accent, the accent of the police, the Special Branch, the detectives, the guards in the jail. They were the accents of authoritarianism, of the officials at the South African embassy with whom he had negotiated all of last week. Negotiated. Pleaded. They were sullen, hostile, showed their dislike and contempt. He had pulled strings. A sympathetic Labor M.P. used influence. A well-placed journalist. His brother-in-law in Capetown, a most eminent psychiatrist with access to many dark secrets, who had aided the troubled child of a South African cabinet minister. A phone call to Pretoria. A favor asked and received. They had stamped his British passport with a visa for one week. Compassionate permission, the clerk at South Africa House said briefly, without compassion. He was traveling six thousand miles to make a week's visit.

The Afrikaans woman beside him finally gave up all

attempts at conversation. She looked up from her *Reader's Digest* disapprovingly when the hostess brought his double whiskey. The alcohol did nothing to loosen the grip on his insides. It merely added a blinding headache, compounding his difficulties. He had hoped the searing scotch would cauterize the image of his family grouped desolate outside the barrier at Heathrow Airport. Not only did they appear more vividly to him, but he became aware of the vastness of continents, oceans, and night that now separated them from him.

The smooth pretty plastic air hostesses all looked as if they had come off the same assembly line, their smiles, politeness, concern, all mass-produced, devised in the same plant. In the front seat, a baby wailed. His dinner was placed before him, as bland and plastic as the girl who served it. He could not eat, asked instead for innumerable cups of coffee.

In his pocket were some sleeping pills. He thought of them with comfort, as some kind of insurance against the nightmare, but could not bring himself to take them.

At Munich they stopped for half an hour. He remained in his seat, with the *British Medical Journal* open on his lap, a bookmark still at the article he had been reading when the phone call had come through from Johannesburg last week. It was still unopened on his lap when the stout lady came back to her seat, complaining that all the shops at the airport were closed and she unable to buy anything, "Ach, not even a cup of coffee, man."

After Munich, blankets and pillows were brought out, lights turned low. Most of the passengers dozed and slept.

He sat bolt upright in his seat in the dimly lit interior of the airplane, the pills still untouched in his pocket. He felt paralyzed by the weight of numbness his anxiety had assumed. His father's deathbed ahead in the brilliance of South African summer. His wife and children behind in the gloom of English winter. Below him the huge African continent, sullen, indifferent, the detachment from the familiar world evoking the unreality of a dream, the throb of the engines assuring it was no dream.

Could it have been any different if he could turn time

back and start again? Sighing, he knew it would be the same. Right down to this moment, he, immobile, in the giant machine that bore him steadily through latitudes and longitudes.

How appropriate for me to be at this point in space and time. Detached. Belonging nowhere. Neither to South Africa where I was born, nor to England where I live. This is the true image of my situation. A point in darkness, neither in one place nor the other.

Even as a child, the feeling of not belonging. The multitude of black faces that always surrounded one. The feeling that it was their country. Grandma always talking of England as "home" and yet, when one got to England, it was also not home. It was their country. One was an outsider there too.

How far back could the blame be laid? To the Christian missionaries bringing the Word to the black heathens? To the imperialist adventurers exploring, exploiting the rich dark continent? To the inquiring seeking spirit of Western man intent on pushing forward the frontiers? How far back can one lay the blame? Where does the tragedy begin? With the dawning of consciousness? With the expulsion from the Garden of Eden?

If one starts to regret, it is a backsliding process, so that the step before each step taken must be regretted. Right down to regretting the fact of one's birth, the existence of the universe. I did what needed to be done. I suppose I would do it again. No change was brought about. A change for the worse, perhaps. . . .

We do what needs to be done. We cannot ask for any guarantees of success. There is no one to issue guarantees.

3

His eyes burned. His neck ached. He released the latch on the seat and leaned back. Sleep would not come. His mind was shot through with misgivings, questions, recollections: images flocked across the field of his consciousness.

Where did it all begin? At what point? Let me remember. Let me try to remember. For ten years it has been put away, a part of my substance, pushed down, out of sight. Ten years. Now there are twelve hours to journey from winter to summer. From night to morning. From darkness to light. Let me try to remember. In this dimly lit cabin high over the northern edge of Africa, try to isolate the points of my involvement. Try to elicit some form, to plot the pattern that brings me to this moment in place and time.

Of one thing he felt certain. His involvement had not come about as the result of a moral or political decision. There had been no soul-searching, no visions, no moment of truth. It had consisted of one small step after another, unnoticed, unplanned.

One small step after another. Starting at the medical school. Yet he had never joined any organization, any group. He had then, had still now, an intuitive distrust, a distaste for political theory, orthodoxy, dogma, party lines. But when there were protest meetings, demonstrations, marches against further erosions into the civil liberties and human rights of black people, he naturally joined them. One did what needed to be done.

He tasted bitterness at the back of his throat remembering the final solemn procession, almost the entire student body of the university, led by gowned and hooded professors, marching in protest against the new education act designed to exclude black students from the universities. In solemn, silent procession they marched. The law was enacted. Black faces disappeared from the campuses: they were shoved into their own, inferior Bantu colleges.

The fist was starting to close while he was still a student, yet in the dailiness of living the pattern was still not apparent.

Later, as a doctor working in a black hospital, he was relieved by the nature of his daily work of the need to fit into a larger philosophical framework. The problems were simplified for him. Here were black people, sick, suffering, in pain. Here was his skill, his knowledge, his compassion. The parts fitted together. They worked.

When there was a necessity to become involved outside the hospital, he merely did what he felt ought to be done. There was the bus boycott. In the dimly lit cabin of the plane he remembered the bus boycott. The ragged bus queues that were a part of his childhood memories, part of the Johannesburg dawn and evening. The lines of black people, threadbare, sleepy, patient. Three hours before they were due in the white kitchens, factories, offices, the ragged queues could be discerned, a shade more substantial than the gray dawn, waiting for the infrequent overloaded buses to trundle them into town. In the late afternoons of his memory, they would form up again on the sidewalks of the prosperous city, weary, endlessly patient, to be carted back to their hovels in the location that festered on the edge of the town, leaving the white residents with only the number of blacks required to maintain them in comfort through the night.

When the bus fares were increased by one penny, their patience ran out. They refused to pay the extra penny; they boycotted the bus service. They walked. Nine miles each way, each day. At dawn through the quiet streets of the suburbs, where houses, swimming pools, tennis courts lay dreaming in large flower-filled gardens. In the evening, weary after the day's labor, they trudged out of the city back to where their shantytown lay under a pall of smoke.

The boycott lasted for three months. He joined other white sympathizers who volunteered to drive boycotters to and from work every day. The police set up road blocks and tried to intimidate the walkers and the volunteers. The blacks were arrested in thousands as they tried to walk to work, for alleged pass or tax offenses. They were fined for giving each other lifts on bicycles. The whites were harassed and threatened. Each morning at dawn he had driven out to the Township, picked up as many as would fill up the car, dropped them in town, gone back for another load, until it was time to be at the hospital. In the evening, after work, he had taxied again. He was stopped by the police daily, his name, address, occupation, license number, noted down by many surly uniformed men wielding stubby pencils in thick fingers, their guns protruding from gleaming leather holsters.

The Africans were not intimidated. The buses stood idle. The effect was felt in the city. On a subsistence diet, walking eighteen miles a day, the workers' efficiency decreased, the commercial life of the city suffered. He remembered the relief, the triumph, when the city council and chamber of commerce finally stepped in to subsidize the penny increase from their own coffers.

A small hard-wrung victory. What needed to be done was done.

The stout woman in the seat beside him snored, moaned in her sleep. Through the small window of the plane he could see flares of light fitfully illuminating the wing. Beyond that, the blackness.

Beyond the blackness, he saw the groups of emaciated farm laborers in Barney's gleaming, well-equipped kitchen. The time of the farm prison scandal. The collusion between the police and the farmers. He remembered his horror, his incredulity, when Barney had first told him that blacks, picked up without their passbooks, arrested for petty offenses, were being offered the choice of trial or a stint of slave labor for a white farmer. He remembered Barney's description of the concentration camp facilities he had seen on some farms, the barracks with concrete bunks, a water pump in the yard, and a latrine for fifty men, a meager diet, dogs and guards to keep them from escaping, locked up each night after work.

From a few who escaped or were released, Barney began to collect evidence. For suits he was bringing against individual farmers, he needed medical evidence about the conditions of the farm prisoners. He needed to work in secrecy. Late at night he would call up. "Paul. How's life, old man? Long time no see. Why don't you and Margot stroll over for a cup of coffee. Una baked one of her fantastic chocolate cakes today."

A few words to Margot. A few instruments slipped into his jacket pocket. A stroll through the quiet of the dark suburb. An occasional African man passing by strumming a rhythmical tune on a cheap banjo, the music dissolving into the high fragrant hedges. Huge gardens separating each sleeping house from its neighbor. Up Barney's tree-lined driveway, the swimming pool reflecting the faintness of the starlight, a syringa tree's creamy breath of heavy perfume.

In the cabin of the airliner his heart lunged painfully at the recollection of the scent of syringa. His mind paced on, unwilling, at this moment, to examine the source of the pain.

Una must have been hanging about in the hall. The front door opened before his finger touched the bell. She said, "Paul, you're an angel. They're in the kitchen." Una, the essential female, leading him through the house; her generous hips and bosom, the well-fleshed solidity of her arms and legs, her brood of children, her cooking and gardening, the density of her being, all anchor and ballast for Barney's dramatic and danger-filled existence.

At the gleaming kitchen table Barney was writing on yellow sheets of foolscap, two black men devouring thick sandwiches of white bread and meat, gulping tin mugs of steaming tea. They looked as if they were covered with ash, the woolly hair, the black of their skin, their shirts made of sugar sacks with slits for head and arms, their ragged trousers, their bare calloused feet, all dusted over with a grayness. And a thin sharp stench that accompanied the grayness. He recognized it. A stench of poverty, deprivation, thin porridge, concrete, metal bars and locks. As he walked in, they stopped eating, gazed uncertainly at Barney to gauge their safety. Barney said, "Paul. You got here quickly, old man." Reassured, they went back to wolfing their food. Una, after a glance at them, started making more sandwiches.

When they could eat no more, he examined them in Barney's study, their filthy knobbly black feet on the fine Persian rugs, the sackcloth shirts against the Liberty chintz fabric of the sofa.

His report the same as the previous batch. The same as further batches. The sparsely fleshed skeletal frames, the darkly pigmented areas of exposed skin, the smoothness of the tongue surface, the swelling of the ankles, all the signs of acute malnutrition. One of the men had scars from whip lashes across his back, partially healed. The other had festering abrasions on his ankle where he said a police dog had grabbed him in an earlier attempt to escape. In the immaculate, pearly tiled powder room, Una helped him wash and bind the man's wounds.

The next afternoon, Una's nursemaid, taking Una's newest baby out in its pram, stopped by in his backyard. From under the coverlet she produced the now typewritten medical report. He interrupted the game of cricket he was having with his two boys to sign the papers and replace them under the baby's pink blanket.

He never weighed up his commitment in a general scheme of things. He merely acted where he felt it necessary

15

to act. Looking back, now, he recognized the pull away from the impotent guilt with which a white child is burdened at his earliest realization that "they" are black and poor and somehow excluded, while one's own whiteness, mysteriously, but undoubtedly, conferred some saving grace.

He remembered his father's kitchen. He, a young child, hearing the adult manservants of the household requesting the note from his parents required by the law if they wished to remain abroad in the town later than midnight. He knew, he had been told, that without the paper scrap of the permission slip, their trusted and beloved servant would land in jail. When he was about twelve years old, he would sometimes write out the permit, the degradation of the situation invading both his own being and that of the black man, old enough to be his grandfather, waiting patiently while the boy laboriously wrote the note at the kitchen table.

He remembered his father going to bail out of jail servants who had been picked up and arrested for not having their passbooks with them.

Later, the humiliation was reenacted with his own children and his own servants. Their gardener would be arrested.

Why is Joseph in jail? the older child would ask.

He went out without his passbook.

Where was his passbook?

He left it in his room.

Why didn't he tell them?

Because he is supposed to carry it with him wherever he goes.

But he only went out to buy cigarettes.

It's a shame.

If Daddy goes out without his passbook he'll be arrested, too.

No. Only black men have to carry passes.

Why?

It's the law.

I thought the law was for protecting people.

This is a bad law.

Can't it be changed?

We'll have to try.

There were many variations on this theme. Margot would say to him, "We can't let the children grow up here, Paul. It's impossible to equate morality with justice. We're all drawn into this shame together, and now the children are starting to ask questions, we have to pull them down with us. We'll have to go and live somewhere else."

From the time of childhood there must have been the unconscious knowledge that one's roots should not be allowed to take hold too fast in the African soil; a self-protective hope that this would make the tearing wrench less painful when its time came.

But in the bright hot sun, in the temperate climate, the roots grew thick, tenacious. His work at the hospital was satisfying and rewarding. He had affection for his black patients; he enjoyed teaching the medical students; he found it stimulating to train his own house physicians. He worked. Read. Listened to music. Played bridge. Watched his children grow. Went on summer vacations to the Cape. Loved his wife. Loved her? In a plane, high above Africa, he found himself considering this for the first time. Yes, loved her, without being too aware of it, probably the way it is in a young marriage that works smoothly.

Life was full, pleasant. There was no clash, no actual confrontation, until the treason trial was over. The treason trial. Barney once again the harbinger of disquieting events. Barney, with whom he had been friends since an afternoon, when he, fifteen years old, was resting beside the school swimming pool after a stint of rigorous practice. He watched the older boy's powerful stroke, insistent, rhythmical, cutting through the water. The boy climbed out, water streaming off the burly muscular form with fine curly red hair covering the chest and limbs, and sprawled down beside him. In the bright sunshine, the chlorinated water of the pool evaporating off their bare bodies, talking of their training, their respective chances in the interschool championships, finding there was

17

no need to explain their terms to each other, that the language of their ideas was similar, some compact was formed that consolidated over the years.

He knew that Barney would be waiting to meet him when the plane landed at the airport in Johannesburg.

Barney had come with his awful information, into their sitting room on an evening when they were drinking coffee after dinner. One hundred and fifty-six people arrested for treason, he announced. A cross section of society, he told them as he drank coffee and puffed at the foul cigars he smoked only when he was agitated, blacks, whites, Indians, coloreds. At dawn that morning they had taken off to jails around the country a group consisting of workers, doctors, students, merchants, lawyers, teachers, a tribal chief, some black housewives from slum dwellings, some white housewives from comfortable middle-class homes. They were all charged with high treason. It's a bad show, Barney said. It's their version of the Reichstag fire. From now on, watch and see, it's going to be intimidation and suppression on a scale we haven't known before. What have these hundred and fifty-six people been doing? They've been talking or writing against apartheid. Or they've been demanding an end to the pass laws, or else they've asked for living wages, education for African kids, decent housing, the right to organize trade unions. All this is high treason. It means that any one of us can be arrested any time now. We're all traitors now.

Barney said, "Paul, old chap, I need your help." They had arrested Benjamin Green, a young lawyer who suffered from chronic heart disease. "We'll have to try and get him out, or at least make sure they treat him properly and let him get his digitalis."

He did whatever Barney suggested was necessary to get Benjamin out of jail, wrote medical certificates, signed affidavits. But the authorities were unconcerned. Benjamin received the same treatment as the others. The straw mattress on the concrete floor, the thin soup and bitter coffee, the lice, the prison yard. They took away his digitalis, and all Barney managed to accomplish was a court order that his medicine be supplied to him.

18

Out on bail for the trial, Benjamin was short of breath, tired, the skin of his twenty-five-year-old face like very old ivory. He knew he was dying, knew his heart would not last out for the dawning of the new day he envisaged for South Africa, but he was elated to be living out his measure of time fighting a battle that gave his life authenticity.

In the years that the treason trial dragged along, with all the accused out on bail and living a precarious existence until the outcome was decided, he got to know Benjamin, and many of the others. Some of them lost their jobs, or their professional practices dwindled because people were afraid to have anything to do with them as long as the indictment hung over their heads. He took care of families who could now not afford to pay their doctors' fees, or whose own doctors now refused to treat them for fear of implicating themselves.

They were all acquitted. The courts, then, were not hamstrung by the legislation that Barney predicted they would pass in order to give the Special Branch power over the judiciary system. There was a victory party. He and Margot were invited. A whole sheep was roasted on a spit over glowing charcoal. The garden was filled with a resinous smell as the marinade was brushed on the turning meat with pine branches. There was an air of elation, champagne. Everyone there—except Barney—thought it was a real victory. Benjamin's eyes glowed and two red spots burned in his white cheeks as he watched his little wife, Lily, who had married him knowing their time together would be brief, dancing barefoot, alone, on the grass under the tall trees, her eyes closed, her dark hair and chiffon dress drifting about her.

Now, she was his little widow Lily, living in London with her two children.

The day after the party was the day of his first visit by the Special Branch. His two detectives that he came to know so well. Laurel and Hardy. Van Niekerk and Bergh. Van Niekerk, a small man with a pinched tight look to him, who spoke seldom, whose manner was distant, official. Bergh, bulky, light on his feet, small eyes with a genial twinkle. A traditional police technique to pair them that way, the grim one to intimidate, the affable one to burrow into one's confidence.

He was making ward rounds with the students when Matron came up to the bedside. She looked anxious. "There are two men to see you in your office, Doctor."

It was unheard of for her to interrupt his rounds. "You'll have to ask them to wait, Matron. I'm in the middle of a ward round."

"I told them you were. They say they have to see you right away. They wanted to come right into the ward but I made them wait in your office."

He asked his senior assistant to continue the round.

His senior assistant, Gilbert. His good friend, Gilbert, who worked now in his department in London; who would run the department for him while he was in South Africa. His good friend Gilbert, who helped Margot and the boys while he was in jail. Who would keep an eye on them this coming week. Whom he had once suspected of betraying him.

Gilbert went on with the ward round. He went to his office where the two men waited. He immediately thought of Laurel and Hardy but felt no desire to smile.

"Good morning, Doctor. We are from the Special Branch. I am Inspector Bergh and this is Sergeant van Niekerk. We wonder if you would mind answering a few questions."

Hardy was humble, respectful. He stood, hat in hand, throughout the interview. Laurel remained seated, glowering, his hat on his head.

"Your car was seen at a certain house last night, Doctor. At a celebration of some sort I believe it was."

"Did you attend the event that took place there?"

"What is your relationship with the occupants of the house?"

"In that case, what were you doing there?"

His answer then, and in all the interrogations that followed later, was, they are patients of mine.

"Would you care to tell us the names of some of the other guests."

He told them he knew hardly anyone there apart from his patient with whom he had come to the party.

Their purpose was to intimidate him. He was not afraid of them. But his mouth was dry, his heartbeat rapid. He felt very alert as if they were opponents in some vital game and he must forestall and outwit them.

Van Niekerk kept riffling through a folder of type-written papers. He felt sure this was another means of inducing fear in him—for all he knew they were sheaves of laundry lists. Van Niekerk was sullen, hostile, a nasty little Stan Laurel. Bergh laughed a lot, obsequiously addressed him as Doctor, thanking him elaborately for his cooperation, making him wonder if he had divulged information inadvertently. Doffing his hat, a large man light on his feet, he took his leave, a jolly Afrikaans-accented Oliver Hardy.

There were a few more encounters with them, apparently pointless.

One, on a Saturday afternoon. Soft brilliant midsummer. He and the boys in the swimming pool splashing about with a huge inflated rubber ball. Margot, in her swimming suit, snipping the heads off spent roses. Suddenly they were there, unannounced, in the green summer garden. Laurel and Hardy, in crumpled cheap suits, hats on their heads.

Scrambling dripping out of the pool, he felt his nakedness as vulnerability beside their fully clothed figures.

Van Niekerk remained silent throughout the interview. Bergh doffed his hat. Manners exquisite, he begged a few moments of the doctor's time. No. There was no need to go indoors, such a beautiful day, though we could certainly use some rain, eh, Doctor. They wouldn't keep him long, just a small routine inquiry. They seated themselves side by side on the garden swing, bizarre in their gray plainclothes on the vivid striped upholstery, shaded by a gaily fringed awning. Margot, beside the pool, watched the boys who went on splashing noisily and happily.

Laurel kept his hat on. Hardy removed his, exposing a red sweaty band round his forehead. He questioned him about his university career, extracted details about all the jobs he had held since he had qualified. He wanted to know where he had spent his last three summer vacations. Then he started a discussion on the advantages and defects of various filter systems for swimming pools. He seemed to have a vast store of knowledge on the subject. Laurel began to fidget, impatient on the striped swing. They took their leave, again with elaborate thanks from Hardy, which again made him feel he had unwittingly given something away.

Margot came up to him, pale under her tanned skin, her eyes made larger by her apprehension.

He reassured her. It is nothing to be worried about. It's an old technique, intimidation. They just want me to know they are watching me. I have done nothing they could even touch me for. Don't worry, darling—forget about them.

The technique worked, though. The summer afternoon was laid over with unease. The garden was seen to be dry. There were more dying than blooming roses. The children started to squabble and Margot sent them to their rooms.

Six months later they visited again, interrupting a dinner party between the main course and the dessert. Leaving the guests uneasy, they interviewed him in his study. I have never belonged to any political organization, he told them. No. Nor that one. Nor that. No. Repeated. I have never been a member of any political organization. Hardy apologized profoundly for interrupting his dinner, hoped the guests would forgive him. He smiled with great charm as he said that in his line of work it was not possible to keep regular hours. Our apologies to your wife and guests.

They left.

The next time he saw them was almost two years later on a morning, before dawn, when they came to arrest him.

4

The interior of the plane was dark and stuffy. He loosened his tie, unbuttoned his collar. He wished he had brought a flask of scotch with him. Looking at his watch he saw that only four hours of the twelve-hour journey had passed. A grip of claustrophobic panic seized him, the same quality of terror with which he had struggled night after night in his dark cell. He could feel himself torn between his terrible reluctance to return to South Africa and his urgent need to see his father.

He slipped past the sleeping bulk of the stout lady and went down the aisle past slumped recumbent forms to the bathroom. He urinated, drank some cold water, avoided his reflection in the mirror. He took out the small phial of sleeping pills, hesitated, put them back in his pocket. No use. He could not submit to their soothing power. He could not let go. He felt he must remain fully in control.

He got back to his seat without waking his companion. He felt his pulse and found it to be racing. He took stock of all the symptoms of anxiety that were manipulating him. He leaned back, resigned to the long night of agony, submitted to it, as to punishment.

Where was I? How did it go from there? In the long vibrating night, he tried to remember.

He remembered Sharpeville.

He remembered the chill as he and Margot heard the announcement of the Sharpeville massacre which interrupted a program of Vivaldi to which they had been listening on the radio. Sharpeville, the broadcast said, a native township thirty miles outside Johannesburg; a crowd of natives demonstrating against the pass laws; fired on by the police; many dead and wounded.

He went back to the hospital. The victims were already being brought in. There were one hundred and eighty wounded and sixty-nine dead. He saw for himself, and later told newsmen, that three-quarters of the victims had been shot in the back. It was no secret.

When he got home, the living room was filled with the smoke of Barney's foul cigars. Barney was slumped in an armchair, heavy with foreboding. Peaceably demonstrating against the pass laws, he told them, unarmed men, women, and kids, the police just opened fire on them, they fled with bullets hailing into their backs. In forty seconds, he mourned, the place was littered with dead and wounded. Remember Guernica? he asked them. This is our Guernica. And watch out now, he warned, this is their glorious opportunity to bring out all their trappings of the police state.

He was right. All the trappings. A state of emergency was declared. Each day they read in the papers of widespread arrests, detention without trial, bannings, restrictions on assembly. A strict censorship was imposed, but, as many people they knew were arrested, they did not need to read the press to know what was happening.

There seemed no logic to their choice of victims. Barney was sure that intimidation was their prime motive, and a show of strength. They needed to appear to be in control of the situation in the eyes of the rest of the world, as Sharpeville had caused foreign investors to doubt the stability

24

of the country, and capital was being withdrawn and the stock market plunging.

Each day they would hear that someone else had been arrested. At three in the morning their cars would draw up, in the white suburbs and the black townships. They would ring or knock, and meticulously proffer arrest warrants to sleepy citizens. They arrested several husbands and wives, allowing them a few minutes to call neighbors or servants in to take care of frightened, crying children.

For months after Sharpeville he acted as general practitioner to temporarily orphaned children who were being looked after by friends or relatives.

He and Margot slept uneasily. A car coming to a stop in their street would startle them awake. Side by side in the dark, they would listen for footsteps on the long verandah. It would turn out to be the carousing son of the next-door neighbor returning home in the small hours, or a doctor making a house call in the quiet neighborhood.

Margot said, again, that they would have to leave, that they could not go on living in this state of fear.

Barney and Una walked over after dinner one night. They all joked about it. You see, we've discovered this trap door under the refrigerator, Barney told them, and if we hear them coming, Una wants me to hide there. But what if they take Una and I'm left to molder under the bloody fridge for years. They all shouted with laughter.

They did not come for Barney. They did not come for him. Their selection seemed random. Its very randomness made it more sinister. They took Harry, Margot's cousin Harry, who had been a Native Representative in the Senate, who for years since losing his seat had devoted himself to a respectable law practice and to studying form at the race course. His wife, Anna, who had been educated at an exclusive girls' school in England dropped in for afternoon tea with Margot. "Harry's been nabbed," she announced.

He remembered how Anna would leave her three children with Margot on visiting days at the jail. On a chilly winter afternoon Margot found all the children playing in the sitting room with a wire-mesh fire screen. They were taking

25

turns visiting each other in jail, the prisoner going behind the fire screen, while the others chatted and brought gifts of sweets and biscuits which they pushed through the wire mesh. Although they all laughed at her wry recounting of the incident, he knew that Margot was deeply disturbed by it.

He gave money to funds that were set up for the families of political prisoners. He was available if a doctor was needed. He went to work every day. He swam in his pool nine months of the year. At dinner parties there was gloomy discussion of the pervading totalitarianism. But the sunshine was generous, benign, the highveld air crystalline, the flowers brilliant, Africans still danced and sang in small groups on street corners at night to their plaintive penny-whistle jazz. It was hard to believe what they all said so glumly to each other.

Some of their friends, taken after Sharpeville, were released. Some remained, under banning orders. Others took exit permits and left the country. At cocktail parties, round swimming pools, at barbecues with white-uniformed servants serving food, there was talk of the growing exile colony in London. In areas of Hampstead, it was said, one heard nothing but South African accents. Shops there were beginning to stock South African foods: *snoek, biltong, granadillas.*

For him, though, that period was overlaid with his love affair with Zainab. He inhaled deeply in the closeness of the plane cabin stuffy with the reused breath of the sleeping passengers. He felt he needed to prime his lungs with extra oxygen if he were to start to think about Zainab. He smelled syringa. A syringa tree had bloomed in his parents' garden when he was seventeen and in love for the first time. When he was thirty-four it was the scent of the perfume that Zainab used. Beneath the smell of ether and disinfectant soap that clung to her at the hospital lay the scent of syringa, as her saris of brilliant silk underlay the starched white fabric of her hospital coat.

The smell of curry. The curries she would cook for him at her flat in Fordsburg. Coming up to her at the stove as she stirred a pot, his mouth on the dark honey of her skin, on her dark hair, he would breathe the fragrance of syringa blended with the pungence of the curried food.

In the two years that they were lovers there were not many opportunities to be alone. At the hospital he saw her every day. Doctor Vaswami, his beautiful senior house physician, second in rank to Gilbert. She had her own flat, but her brother Ahmed had used a small room there as a meeting place for his activities on the Indian National Congress. On the wall there had been a large picture of Gandhi. Beneath it Ahmed had pinned a hand-printed sign. Gandhiji. Who Founded The Natal Indian Congress In 1894. Who Lived One Block Away From These Premises In 1897.

The plane lurched sickeningly. Lights flashed on. Fasten your seatbelts. Fasten your seatbelts. The air hostesses appeared, woke sleeping passengers, helped buckle seatbelts. The pilot's voice came over the loudspeakers, announcing some slight turbulence, advising passengers to remain in their seats with their belts fastened, informing them that they were three hours out of Nairobi, that they would land there at six A.M., that they would stop there for one hour.

The flurry of excitement died down. The baby in the front seat whined. The hostess came past with a nursing bottle of milk. The baby quieted. Lights were turned low. People slept and snored again.

Infinitely weary, he dozed. Dreamed. Dreamed he was in Zainab's flat. She wandered about brown and naked, slender but as extravagantly curved as a figure in erotic Hindu temple sculptures. He smelled a compound of ether, syringa, curry. In Ahmed's small room, on a striped garden swing, Laurel and Hardy sat in crumpled gray suits under a large poster of Gandhi. Ahmed sat at a table with some Indian and African men. One of the Africans looked up, his eyes insolent, invasive, slidingly shifty. He was the man who had been with Abel Mashaba and the wounded man at Illovo.

He struggled back to wakefulness, his heart pumping, sweat beading out on his lips and forehead. That face, the sliding glance. He felt the dark cabin closing in on him. He unfastened his seatbelt and stood up. A little air hostess appeared and told him sharply to remain in his seat, to fasten his belt.

He obeyed, tried to regain control, told himself, too many sleepless nights, tension, anxiety, reawakening of old fears. The agitated racing of his pulse slowed down. He wiped the chilling sweat off his face. His head throbbed. The air hostess came by and regarded him suspiciously. He asked for aspirin, swallowed it down with water that she brought in a flimsy paper cup.

Over the wing of the plane a dark patch detached itself from the night and moved toward the window. The black face. It must have been that one. He had gone over it a thousand times. All the nights of solitary confinement. The first years in London after his release. That black face lurked in his sleep. It must have been that one.

In the servants' quarters of the house in Illovo, there had been the wounded man; there had been Ahmed, now living in exile in Tanzania; there had been Abel Mashaba, now in jail; there had been Barney; and that other face with the sliding eyes. How else could they have known that he had been there that night? The man must have been working with the police.

One o'clock in the morning. The tapping on the bedroom window. Through the glass, Barney's moon face, his pale red hair awry. "Let me in, man." The hasty conference in the hall. A wounded African, Barney told him, a bullet wound, weak, seems to have lost quite a bit of blood, Ahmed and Mashaba have brought him to some place in Illovo. Apprehension in Margot's eyes, but, as always, she was efficient, intelligent, anticipating his requirements, getting his bag, his instruments, a flask of brandy, while he dressed.

A moonless night, so dark that, when he later told Laurel and Hardy that he had no idea where the house was, he spoke the truth.

In a room in the servants' quarters of an Illovo country estate, a black man moaning on a pile of blankets. An African supporting the head of the wounded man, holding a mug of water to his lips, whose eyes slid over him like a lizard's as he came in with Barney. Ahmed gripped his shoulder, comrade-ly, relieved he had come. Abel Mashaba, a schoolteacher he had met once at Zainab's flat, who said, "Doctor, thank God you are here."

He remembered that as he examined the patient, Barney had gone outside and peed loudly in the shrubbery. Had come in again fastening his fly. The wound was clean. The bullet had passed right through the flesh of the thigh. By now the bleeding had stopped. He dressed the wound, gave the man an injection of pethidine for the pain. Someone emptied the water from the tin mug, and he poured brandy into it. The man drank, coughed, spluttered, grinned, said, "Man. I feel better already." They all laughed. "Did you bleed very much?" Not too much, Doctor, someone at Alexandra Township gave me a clean pair of trousers. It's the pain."

"I've given you something for the pain. Here are some pills in case it gets bad again. One every four hours. Try to keep it clean. Here are extra dressings, antiseptic. If it starts to swell or discharge, or if you notice any swelling, here, in your groin, you must get to a doctor. Good luck."

The man gripped his hand in both of his own. "Thank you, Doctor. I appreciate your goodness."

He and Barney left. The whole thing took fifteen minutes.

Driving back through the deserted suburban streets, he remembered saying to Barney, "When people need doctors, they invest us with a kind of priestly function. It fills me with humility. All we have is access to a few techniques. And we are as vulnerable as they are."

Barney said, "Sorry, old man. Whether you like it or not—if a man is afraid that his life is dripping away through a little hole in his flesh, and you step between him and his fear of death, your function *is* a priestly one. For him you possess magic powers. You *are* invulnerable."

That was the only conversation they had. He did not ask Barney about the wounded man, and Barney offered no explanations.

5

He did not feel invulnerable a few weeks later, when he answered the doorbell's strident ring at three in the morning to find Laurel and Hardy standing on the verandah.

"Sorry to disturb you, Doctor. I wonder if you would mind coming along with us to the station to answer a few questions."

Margot's eyes were somber in her ashen face. The children went on sleeping. He went into his bedroom and dressed, came back to the sitting room. Laurel sat rigid on a chair, hat on head. Hardy's hat was on the piano, he wandering about examining their paintings and drawings with curiosity.

Hardy looked up at him and said, "Oh, by the way, Doc, maybe you should pack a few things, you know, pajamas, shaving gear."

"I thought you said we were just going for questioning."

Laurel stood up. "Don't waste our time, Doctor. You heard what he said."

Margot went back to the bedroom with him. Margot, in her long blue tailored dressing gown neatly tied at the waist, her short hair glossy and kempt even though she had just been rudely wakened. In her soft kid slippers she moved quietly about packing his things for him. The book that lay open on his bedside table—*Middlemarch*—his pipe, tobacco pouch, all packed into a small calf leather overnight bag with his initials stamped on it in gold. She snapped the bag closed. They looked at each other. She said, "Don't worry about us. We'll be all right. Just take care of yourself." She said, "I'll phone Barney."

Little Margot. Just five feet tall. So neatly put together in body and soul. A small formidable person, straight with strength and devotion.

They returned to the sitting room.

He left with Laurel and Hardy. He felt absurd. His complete lack of choice in his circumstances made him feel absurd. On the verandah he said to Margot, "Don't forget to bolt the door."

She said, cheerful for the benefit of the two detectives, "See you soon, darling."

They did not see each other again in South Africa. Months later they met again in London. Only then did she allow herself to let go of her control. At Heathrow Airport, when he came through the customs barrier, thinner, his hair a lot grayer, she held on to him and wept. A small, brave woman, neatly put together in body and soul. She did not squander her spirit; she conserved it, requiring it for the survival of her children and herself. Only when they were all safe again, together, did she indulge in the luxury of weeping.

6

In the driveway a plain black car was parked, with a plainclothes driver. Discreet, the Special Branch. They took care not to shame one in front of the neighbors with uniforms and police cars.

He sat in the back between Laurel and Hardy. Hardy said, "Nice little woman your wife."

He made no attempt to respond. Wave after wave of fear of a kind he had never known, washed over him. When Hardy had told him to pack his bag, a fearful thought had transfixed him. They had come for him because they knew about Zainab.

In the car, his apprehension burned and chilled him. The Immorality Act. Their legislation invades even sexual relationships. Headlines. White Doctor and Indian Doctor Found Guilty Under Immorality Act. Admit Having Sexual Relations. Both Sentenced. He thought of Zainab's quietness. He thought of Margot, trim, neat, in her blue dressing gown; the bewilderment of his children. His father. He saw Barney's moon face with its sad gentle expression surrounded by a halo of unkempt red hair. Sweat ran down from his armpits, from the small of his back. He saw his involvement with a beautiful intelligent Indian girl turning sordid and grimy in the sick flare of publicity. What about Ahmed, and Zainab's parents, to whom their emancipated daughter was a source of such pride? He thought, what if they have taken Zainab too. He felt ice forming in his chest. He saw every action he had ever taken in his life as worthless, meaningless.

At the police station, they fingerprinted him. They removed his watch, pen, money, tie, belt. They took him to a comfortably furnished office where a distinguished-looking man, gray-haired, in immaculate uniform, introduced himself as Colonel van Reenen, invited him to sit down, offered him coffee. When it reached him that they were questioning him about treating a wounded kaffir in Illovo, his relief thawed his chilled blood, started it moving again.

He drank the coffee they gave him, and in the wake of what seemed for the moment to be a reprieve, he felt an access of strength that would enable him to withstand them. Although they had taken a measure of his self-sufficiency away by removing his tie and belt and personal possessions, he did not feel intimidated. He gave them his usual approach.

"I am a doctor, Colonel. I have a duty to minister medical aid when I am called. If someone needs help, I am obliged to give it."

The colonel was charming, excessively polite. He spoke perfect English, with a heavy Afrikaans accent. Laurel and Hardy lurked about near the window, coming up to the desk occasionally to talk in undertones to the colonel.

"But, Doctor, we have reason to believe that the wounded kaffir belongs to a revolutionary organization that functions outside our borders. An organization which is dedicated to the overthrow of our republic. We do not feel you did wrong giving him care, as a responsible doctor. As a responsible citizen of the republic, however, you should have reported the matter to the police."

"I have a responsibility to my patients. There is such a thing as privilege between doctor and patient that I cannot betray."

"What was the name of this kaffir you treated?"

"I neither asked nor was I told."

"Where was he coming from?"

"I have no idea."

"Where was he heading for?"

"I don't know."

"What did you do for him?"

"I dressed an injury and gave him an injection for pain."

"What was the nature of his injury?"

"I cannot disclose my patient's confidence."

The colonel offered him a cigarette from a silver box on the desk. He declined. The colonel helped himself, lit up, inhaled luxuriously, gazed up at the ceiling, and emitted a few expert smoke rings. Hardy looked on with admiring humility, Laurel remained stone faced. The gray cloud of smoke hung above the desk between them.

"We happen to know, Doctor, that the kaffir was treated for a bullet wound."

He remained silent.

"Tell me, Doctor, how did you become aware of this kaffir's need for first aid?"

All the implications of the situation, obscured by the earlier, misdirected fear, presented themselves to him. The wave of confidence began to subside.

He said, "Colonel. Isn't it customary for a person to have access to a lawyer before being interrogated?"

"Not when that person is being detained under the Ninety Day Act, Doctor. If we wish it, you will have no access, *no access*, you follow me? to *anyone whatsoever* for ninety days." He smiled with charm. "If, on the other hand, you are prepared to cooperate with us by answering a few simple questions, you will be home in time to have breakfast with your wife and your two little boys."

Breakfast with his wife and two little boys. The colonel's words evoked with vividness what now seemed the most remarkable event in his existence. Breakfast with his

34

wife and two little boys. The morning sun lighting up the jar of marmalade. The boys, their shining early morning faces, the older neat in his school uniform, both intent on their bowls of cereal. Margot, tidy in her blue dressing gown, pouring tea, buttering toast, the economy of her movement. In the silence, he looked around the room, saw Laurel and Hardy leaning against the wall, hollow men, their spiritual aspirations so paltry that they would serve any master, march to any beat, achieving perhaps some kind of shabby satisfaction at the exercise of their thirdhand power. His breakfast table faded away, as remote and inaccessible as a vision of paradise.

"Would you care for some more coffee, Doctor?"

"No thank you."

"Would you like to tell us then, so that we can get this little matter over with as soon as possible, how you received the message to go to the wounded kaffir? This in no way infringes the—ah—bounds of your professional ethics."

Barney. Ahmed. Abel Mashaba. He always made a point of knowing as little as possible. Even so, he already knew too much.

It occurred to him then that if they knew he was at Illovo, they also knew who else was there. They were playing cat and mouse with him.

He said. "I was asked to see a patient. I cannot say by whom."

"How did you get there?"

"I was driven."

"By whom?"

"I cannot say."

"Can you tell us the address?"

"I don't know the address. It was a dark night and I couldn't see where we were going."

"When you got there who else was there?"

"There were two or three other men."

"Kaffirs? Whites? Indians?"

"It was dark. My only interest was with the patient. I don't know who the others were. There were a few figures in the dark."

The colonel stood up, stubbed out his cigarette in a heavy glass ashtray. A charming, urbane Afrikaner. He said, "Well, Doctor. Perhaps a few days of solitary—shall we say, contemplation—might serve to refresh your memory."

Looking back on it from here, from ten years, from high up in a black sky, he knew he had had a pretty easy time of it in jail. Later, in London, talking to the others, he heard about experiences of physical and psychological brutality. The black political prisoners were tortured. He was mostly left alone. For seventy-one days.

After a week, they gave him back his copy of *Middlemarch*. He read it over and over. It stood up to many rereadings. A fine book to be thrown into jail with. It touched and amused and affected him; it provoked contemplation; its irony supported him when he tended to take his situation too narrowly, too literally, reminded him that there was a whole world of moral existence beyond the sphere inhabited by the colonel, Laurel and Hardy, the prison guards.

At the second interview a week later, Laurel and Hardy lurked, the colonel was bluff, man to man.

"I am going to be perfectly frank with you, Doctor. You are an intelligent man, there is no need for me to beat about the bush. You realize, of course, that we know perfectly well what happened that night at Illovo. We know exactly who was there. Now then. We have an important trial coming up. Important for the security of the republic. It will have to be made quite obvious to the whole of Africa that we *cannot and will not* tolerate these black communist terrorists and revolutionaries infiltrating our borders to sow the seeds of dissent and revolt in our country. Now then, Doctor. What we want you to do is give evidence for the state. You will be compromising no one, because all the co-conspirators are not only known to us, but are already in our hands."

Ahmed? Mashaba? Do they have them? Barney? Did they take him too?

"Now, Doctor. If you will merely answer these few questions, Inspector Bergh here will take your statement and type it out for you to sign, we will return your personal possessions to you, and you will be free to go home."

He said, "Colonel, my answer is the same as before. I administered medical aid to a man who was hurt. Further than that there is nothing I can tell you."

The colonel remained suave, unperturbed. They could have been at a cocktail party.

"Very well, Doctor. Thank you. That will be all for now."

His guard had removed the laces from his shoes. He turned to go out of the colonel's office, his shoes scuffing. As he reached the doorway, the colonel remarked, casually, as an afterthought, "You realize, of course, that you can be detained indefinitely for withholding evidence."

He did not see Laurel and Hardy again. From then on, he was the colonel's.

He learned how, between an interrogator and his victim, there develops a strange, complex relationship; a delicate balance, like the tension that exists between two lovers. Whenever he was fetched for questioning, he would feel a quickening, of fear, of hope, of elation, of despair, a state not unlike that with which he used to anticipate a meeting with Zainab; an increased animation, a surging outward of responsiveness.

"Ah, good morning, Doctor. And how are you? Everything all right I hope. Any complaints?"

He would have made a good headwaiter.

If he complained of an insufficiency of blankets, inadequate exercise period, his requests were granted. But apart from *Middlemarch*, the colonel allowed him no reading matter, no visitors, no mail, no communications at all with the outside world.

He yearned, miserably, for his pipe and tobacco.

The colonel never lost his patience, always remained good tempered. "You must realize, Doctor, that you are keeping yourself in prison. Make half a dozen simple statements for us and you are free to leave."

He would return to his cell, his laceless shoes making his

walk ungainly. But when the spring of tension unwound, he would fall into blackness. Yet, if a week passed by and he was not called for interrogation, he felt spurned, ostracized.

He could see the form of the colonel's plan steadily to demoralize him, to undermine the connection he still sensed with the outside orderly world. "Are you not aware, Doctor, that you are being used by these people, that you are merely a pawn in their scheme to seize power and disrupt the republic with violence and dissension? And now that you are no longer of use to them, as far as they are concerned you are a forgotten man." The colonel looked at him with what seemed to be genuine sympathy and concern. "Just look at yourself, Doctor, you are falling apart—you are not the man you were when you were brought in here a few short weeks ago. How can it be worth it to you to suffer like this for people who consider you expendable, who have already forgotten you?"

Though his intelligence would stand aside and scorn the colonel's expert technique, another part of him, anterior to intelligence, began to feel the erosion.

At the beginning, he thought they would probably let him go when the ninety days were up. So long as there was a shape to his time in prison he felt able to cope with it. Then one day he remembered a story Barney had told him about a journalist whom they had released on the ninetieth day, only to rearrest her in the telephone booth outside the jail where she was phoning her husband and children to come and fetch her.

There followed panic, with its claustrophobic quality that became his nightly attendant; then hopelessness and the belief that everyone had in fact forgotten him; then a terrible desire to tell the colonel his meager tale, and leave. He spent long hours persuading himself. After all, what harm could it do now. He was convinced that they knew everything, that his puny scrap of evidence could hurt no one. His nights were torn through with dreams of Margot and the children being overtaken by nameless disasters, while he, sinking into heavy mud, or plunging down precipices, or finding his legs paralyzed, was unable to help them.

Finally he convinced himself that his responsibility to his wife, his children, his patients, made it necessary for him to get out of jail. He would harm no one by telling the little he knew. He went to two interviews determined to give them their statement, but when actually confronted with the colonel found himself unable to do it. Then, after a week of terrible nights, the claustrophobia at his throat, the skin of his body electrified with needle shocks of fear, he decided he would tell the colonel he was prepared to cooperate at their next session.

He was brought in for his interview. He had been in his cell, alone, for seven weeks. The colonel was freshly barbered, smelled of a sharp masculine cologne; a crisp white handkerchief was tucked into his sleeve. He poured two cups of coffee.

But instead of going through their usual routine like well-rehearsed actors familiar with their lines, the colonel said immediately, "Well, Doctor, we have some news for you today."

He waited, his coffee untouched, feeling the blood fall in his heart.

"Some news of your wife and sons."

The skin crawled on the back of his arms and neck.

"I'm afraid, Doctor, that your charming wife has—shall we say—deserted you. Decamped. Run off. Abandoned you to your fate."

He's lying. It's obvious that he's lying. He's trying to frighten me. He waited, feeling he held the advantage if he kept his silence.

The colonel took a small nail file from his pocket and filed a corner of a shiny pink manicured nail. He kept on filing as he spoke. "We have information that your wife has taken your two boys and run off to England with another man. It seems that she, like us, has run out of patience with you, Doctor."

He stood up pushing his chair back. "You're lying of course, Colonel. You're trying to break me down."

The colonel looked shocked. "My dear Doctor! We have the facts. She has been seen constantly in the company of this man who accompanied them on the plane to London. She is living with him in a flat in London right at this moment."

In the weeks that followed he knew that if they had not removed his tie, his belt, if they had provided him with sheets, he would have tried to kill himself. What he experienced in this period was life at such a worthless level that existence itself was an act of negation. He began to feel that there was something shameful about the fact of his being: it would be better for Margot and the boys if he could just be expunged. It was as though he had a hideous shameful disease and his existence was a source of embarrassment and humiliation to his family.

Later, he sank into a pit of guilt. He was being punished. This could not be an action of contingency. He was being punished to level out the balance. Life had been too easy up till now. The human condition is not supposed to be this way. To be human is basically a tragic condition. Now he must pay. The balance must be restored. He had had a happy childhood. He walked around and around the periphery of his cell, weighing and measuring out his guilt. His parents: his father, a mild physician, his mother, a vital energetic painter; they had provided whatever a child's spirit needed to enrich and brace it. He derived a deep satisfaction from his work. He had a charming and intelligent wife; his two sons were a source of constant wonder. It was too much, too much bounty for one man. And as if this were not enough, he had Zainab. Zainab, who, with her extraordinary beauty, combined the incisiveness of Western wit and intelligence with an Eastern acceptance of intuitive wisdom that went beyond science and rationality.

Now the surfeit was being redressed. Now he had nothing. Everything that had ever had value or joy for him was turned to ash. In the days that followed, a part of him registered amazement that he, Paul, could inhabit such a region of wretchedness. I could have gone my whole life, he thought, without ever knowing that I had this capacity, this talent, for pain and hopelessness.

When he found he was left with nothing, he discovered

that there was one last thing he could hold on to. His silence. If I have nothing else left, I have this. I won't give it up to them. They can keep me here forever, for an indeterminate number of ninety-day periods, but they are not going to get what they want from me. He knew that now it was not a matter of principle, of heroics; it was no longer a matter of not betraying his friends. It was the only single thing he had left. It was his reason for existence.

He scarcely touched any food. He stopped reading George Eliot. He lay about on his bunk all day. Strangely, he had long uninterrupted periods of sleep at night. It was as though he had disciplined himself to stop dreaming, like a man trapped in a cave trying to conserve his oxygen. He grew thin, shaved only because the guards ordered him to, stood leaning against the courtyard wall till his exercise period was over.

Just outside the prison walls was the bustling suburb of Hillbrow: shops, cinemas, cafes, the medical school where he had studied, housewives shopping, nursemaids pushing babies in prams. He was as removed from it all as he was from the mountains of the moon.

At his interviews with the colonel, he was uninterested, apathetic. His knowledge that he would not tell became as much a part of him as his breathing. He had no need to think about it anymore.

On the seventy-first day, after lunch, a guard came in with his clothes and told him to get dressed. His heart did not stir. He expected nothing. He dressed and was taken to the colonel's office. On the desk lay his wallet, his watch, his pen, his pipe and tobacco pouch, his leather bag. The colonel, cold, distant, told him to check his possessions, gave him a receipt to sign.

He did as he was told, listless, apathetic. A young policeman packed his possessions into the bag with initials worked on in gold.

The colonel stood up, hostile, withdrawn.

He thought, we are like lovers who have quarreled.

"Doctor. You may go. I must inform you, however, that your house has been searched and your passport removed.

41

You are no longer entitled to the privilege of the protection invested in the passport of the republic. You will, however, be granted an exit permit, which means you are free to leave the republic, but, should you ever return, you will be placed immediately under arrest." He leaned forward, his long elegant fingers resting on the desk, his handsome features slightly altered by a vicious expression that flickered and was gone. "I would advise you, for your own good, to be out of the country in seventy-two hours." He withdrew into a stony abstraction.

He picked up his bag and followed the young policeman down a corridor, through a lobby. The policeman pushed open a heavy studded door and stepped aside to let him pass. He went down the steps, out into the street.

7

Outside, it was a fine brilliant autumn day. He stood on the street corner. The sunlight made his eyes ache, the noise of the traffic assaulted his hearing. He felt as if he were an invisible man, as if he were watching the bustling activity of the city but no one could see he was there.

A memory nudged him. They had rearrested the woman journalist in the telephone booth a yard from where he stood. The first small current, a recognition of a desire for survival, galvanized him. He moved quickly away from the prison.

He walked along the crowded main street of Hillbrow until he came to a telephone booth. He went in and stood looking out. No one seemed the least bit interested in him. He took a coin from his pocket, and then his frame was shaken by a chill of trembling. Who should he phone? He thought, my spirit is being restored to me in spurts of terror and cowardice. His hand shook so that it was difficult for him to dial the number of his house. The phone rang and rang. He could see it ringing on his desk in the study, on his bedside table. He wondered what day it was. Perhaps it was the servants' day off, Margot out shopping, the children at school.

He knew all along that the colonel had not been lying. He could hear the phone was ringing in a deserted house. He replaced the receiver. His coin was returned. He stared out at the sunny crowded streets, at the shopwindows filled with goods, at the very ordinariness of the day outside the glass walls of the telephone booth.

He inserted the coin again, dialed a number. Una's voice emerged, warm, assuasive, from her buxom chest and well-fleshed throat.

"Hullo."

"Una."

"Who's that?"

"Paul."

The silence hummed along the line.

"Paul! Darling, where are you?"

"In a phone booth in Hillbrow."

"Listen to me darling. Go into Florian's and buy yourself a cup of coffee. I'll be there in fifteen minutes."

This was what he wanted. He had been passive for so long that he was incapable of making a decision.

He went into the espresso bar and ordered cappuccino. While he waited, a nurse he knew came in. "Hullo, how are you, Doctor? Long time no see. What are you doing in a coffee bar on a Wednesday afternoon anyway? I thought every doctor in town was out on the golf course." She looked around at all the tables. "I'm supposed to be meeting my sister here—she must be in the other room. See you, Doctor." He watched her stride off, her uniformed waist cinched in by a broad canvas belt.

He felt surprised she had spoken to him. He still felt invisible.

He changed his seat so that his back was turned to the cafe. So it was Wednesday today. The waiter brought a frothing mug of cappuccino. He sipped it slowly. The steaming fragrance, sweet, creamy, with a hint of bitterness, was new, surprising to his grateful palate. He thought, sensation is returning to the patient.

Behind him there was a rustling and a breathing, a warm female scent. Una was encompassing him in ample arms to her abundant bosom, her plump cheek against his. She said, "Paul, Darling. Come quickly, I've double parked and I've got two kids and the dog and the lawn mower in the car."

In the car, she squeezed his hand and they drove back in silence, the children, wide-eyed, regarding him with awe.

Barney had come home by the time they got there.

As he got out of the car he noticed the grass was yellowing, red and brown leaves floated on the surface of the swimming pool. In the living room the fire burning in the grate was reflected in copper jugs, warming pans, fire irons, horse brasses. There were vases filled with zinnias and chrysanthemums.

Barney hugged him, stepped back to look at him, said, "First of all," and fetched him a tumbler filled with scotch and ice.

They all sat down round the fireplace. Barney said, "And second of all, you know, I presume, that Margot and the kids are safe in London."

His hand shook so that the ice rattled noisily about in the glass. He took a long searing pull at the whiskey, and asked, "What . . . what happened to them?"

"You understand, Paul—they were keeping a watch on Margot. We thought they might take her, and then use this as a threat to you. We were worried about the kids. So we decided the best thing would be for her to get out. Your father and Gilbert and I arranged it. Gilbert was an angel. Phoned his sister Moira in London to meet them and put them up till they could find a place of their own. They stayed with her for a month till they found a flat. The boys are in school and Margot's got a decent job at a children's library in Hampstead."

"Who's with them?" He had not used his voice for so long it came out gruff, rusty.

"Who's with them? What d'you mean old chap?"

"Don't try to save my feelings, Barney. It's all right. I know. Colonel van Reenen told me."

"Told you? What did he tell you, old chap?"

He could not look at Barney and Una. He looked down at the hearthrug. He spoke in a low voice. "He told me she's gone off with someone. She's living in London with someone. Who is it? Is it Gilbert?" His face burned with his shame.

He looked up, saw Barney and Una exchange shocked glances. They stared at him.

"He told you that?" Barney said.

He did not know how much he was shaking until he felt the chill of the whiskey spilling over his hand, his trouser leg. He put his glass down on the hearth.

Barney repeated. "He told you that?" He held his arms a little away from his body, clenched his beefy fists that were covered with curly red hair. His face was suffused with blood. He held his head up as though he were about to address a large crowd. He said, "Oh, the lousy bastards. Oh, what lousy, swinish bastards they are."

Una said, "Paul. D'you mean to say. D'you mean, all the time you were in there—in solitary—you thought! Oh, darling."

Una always wore smocks, like a nursery school teacher, with capacious pockets filled with a variety of small objects, tools, sweets, string, crayons, dog biscuits, clothespins. She scrabbled in a pocket, took out a large, checked man's handkerchief, shook it open, covered her face with it, and wept loudly.

Una wept. He and Barney drank scotch. No one tried to console her. There was no consolation available for any of them. He felt shamed by his situation, as he had felt in his prison cell, as though he were covered with festering sores.

Eventually, Una blew her nose. Barney said, "Una, see if you can get hold of Paul's father and tell him he's out."

In the cozy sitting room, they sat, silent. The fire and the scotch burned steadily, comfortingly. Una came back. "I spoke to Rosie. Your dad's playing golf. He'll be back at five."

For an instant he felt deeply wounded, self-pitying. Dad plays golf while I languish in jail. Then it occurred to him that even if he had died, there would be no point in his father giving up his game of golf. Life goes on. He had an image of life as an eternally spinning merry-go-round. Either you're on, or you're off, it stops for no one. Dully he thought, I have to try and get back on. It seemed to spin so violently, so pointlessly, that he doubted if he had the strength or even the desire to get back on.

He said, feeling a great weariness, "Barney, Colonel van Reenen told me I have to be out of the country in seventy-two hours."

"Seventy-two hours! Oh, the lousy swinish bastards. Seventy-two hours. OK, Paul. Let's see what we have to do then. Jesus Christ. Seventy-two hours."

8

"Ladies and gentlemen. Attention please. Attention please. In precisely thirty minutes we will be landing at Nairobi Airport. Passengers disembarking at Nairobi, please have your vaccination certificates and customs declarations ready. All other passengers are requested to leave the airplane for at least half an hour so that the cabin can be sprayed. Thank you."

Outside the small windowpane the night was turning gray and pearly with the dawn. It became light rapidly. Lights were turned off in the plane. Far below, between the clouds, he caught glimpses of red-brown stretches of arid earth, then land masses covered with dense bush which sheltered the lion, elephant, giraffe which must be stirring now in the Kenya dawn. Africa sprawled out beneath them.

"Seventy-two hours." Those last seventy-two hours were telescoped into a series of dreamlike images, unreal, empty of emotional content; himself, going through a succession of motions; doing as he was told.

There was Barney, driving him to his father's house, bringing him up to date. This one under house arrest; that one banned; another one detained indefinitely in jail; someone else had escaped over the border and was living in Ghana; a story about Margot to which he listened dully. Months later, in England, when Margot retold it in her dry, laconic fashion, he was able fully to savor it. "Margot," Barney said, "what a terrific broad she is. You see, she was taking care of Dorothy's children for the afternoon while Dorothy went to visit Max at the Pretoria jail. Dorothy had mentioned that she'd found some papers of Max's—some P.A.C. stuff, some copies of the Freedom Charter—and had shoved them in the piano bench until she had a chance to get rid of them. Anyway, at teatime, the kids were all out in the backyard with the nanny, and Margot was in the kitchen making tea, when two Special Branch bastards pitched up with a search warrant. Margot told them—you know how cool she can be—that she was busy with the children, that it wasn't her house, and she could give them no assistance whatever. Then, while they were searching the study, she calmly took the papers from the piano bench, slipped them into a music book, Czerny's studies she said it was." Barney chuckled at the recollection. "Then she went out and called Dorothy's kids and said, come on darlings, time for your music lessons. The older kid began to protest that they didn't have a lesson that day; the younger one was indignant because he hadn't had his tea yet. But Margot just steamrollered the poor kids. She said to the nanny, all right Johanna, they're ready, off you go. She whispered to the nanny to take the kids to the park and not to come back as long as the S.B. car was parked outside the house. The nanny caught on, and they went off carrying all that hot stuff in the music books. The cool nerve of that Margot. I tell you, Paul, she's a girl in a million."

At his father's house, Rosie opened the front door. Old Rosie, who had been working for his family since before he was born. Who figured in his earliest memories. Like so many South African whites, he had had two mothers, a white one and a black one. His mother's face and Rosie's were the first two faces he knew, hovering over his cradle, his crib, his bed. Rosie, pushing him in his pram to the park every afternoon, in her blue overall and starched white apron and cap. Rosie, sitting on a park bench marked Non-Europeans Only, while her small white charge played in the sandbox, splashed in the paddling pool, swung, seesawed, comparing with the other black nannies in the park the achievements of her little white master. All the black nannies spending their maternal feelings on the small white children they tended, their own black babies away in the *kraals* being taken care of by elderly grandmothers. Rosie had never had children. She had Solly, her nephew who had been born with two clubfeet. She saw to Solly's medical requirements, his education. Although she was fond of her nephew, Paulie, her small white master, was closer to her heart. She had walked him to school and fetched him each day when he was too young to go on his own. She had sung Xosa songs to him and comforted him on her broad lap, had washed and ironed his clothes, baked his birthday cakes. When her white mistress had died, Rosie went on running the house as she had always done, her maternal role long established.

Old Rosie opened the front door. She said, "Master Paul. Oh, Paulie—what did they do to you?" She covered her face with her snowy apron and cried. He put his arms about her, tried to comfort her. "I'm all right, Rosie, I'm all right." But he felt nothing.

Dad came out of the living room. Tall, handsome, with his head of white hair. He said, "Paul. Thank God." He embraced him, blew his nose loudly, patted weeping Rosie.

He thought, everywhere I go people start crying.

For seventy-two hours he was a son again. Not a man, not a husband, not a father, not a physician. He did as he was told. He slept in his old room. Rosie, glad to have him to herself again, hovered over him, cooked his favorite food, forced him to eat. He left his plates clean and empty like an obedient boy. She gossiped with him, about Solly, about Solly's wife and children, about poor Miss Margot and the children alone in London. She worried about his loss of weight.

Barney and Dad arranged everything. Exit permit. Plane booking. Packers to crate his household effects and ship them to England. Estate agents to sell the house. Barney explained the currency limitations. He listened, agreed, signed forms without reading them. None of it was real.

The only reality was the darkness he carried about within him. He was aware of it constantly, with a fearfulness that went beyond the horror of his incarceration, beyond the wretchedness of those weeks when he had believed that Margot had abandoned him, beyond the shattering of his peaceful existence. The knowledge of black reaches in himself, the presence of which he had not sensed; a dark continent he had discovered his being contained, which he knew, now, he would carry about with him always.

Passive, he did what they suggested, agreed with whatever they planned for him. Una went with him one afternoon to his own house to collect some clothes and documents. She was anxious about the effect the place would have upon him. But it did not touch him, the house where he and Margot had lived for ten years, where the two boys had been born. The inner blackness prevailed and he could feel nothing else. The house did not touch him. He was a non-person in a nonhome with a nonfamily. There was, though, one brief flick of pain at the sight of his younger son's tricycle parked neatly in the garage. Dully, he knew he would live again.

He made no attempt to get in touch with Zainab.

On the Saturday night, leaving Rosie, his black mother, crying in the kitchen, he left for the airport with Dad and Barney and Una. Gilbert was there too, to say good-bye. They were a sorry little party. No one said much. There was nothing much to say. He still felt shameful, like a leper. With relief he went up the gangway onto the plane, cradling his darkness tenderly inside him. Not declaring it. Smuggling it out of the country. Smuggling it into England.

Early next morning, Margot was waiting to meet him at London Airport. When he came through the immigration barrier, thinner, a lot grayer, she held onto him, and wept. A small brave woman, neatly put together in body and soul, she did not squander her spirit. She conserved it, requiring it for the survival of her children and herself. Only when they were all safe again, together, did she indulge in the luxury of tears.

PART TWO

9

At Nairobi Airport the airliner bounced softly down and slowed to a halt on African soil.

He waited in his seat till most of the passengers were off. He loosened his belt, stretched his cramped limbs, went down the gangway onto the airfield.

Halfway between the plane and the squat airport building he was overcome by a sensation, sharp and vivid, so that he stopped in his tracks and could not move. It assailed him like a cramp. It was as though he had been assaulted by an axe blow of knowledge, not from the head but from the gut. It was Africa. It came to him as he breathed in the sharp, pristine aridity of the huge continent. As he stood there, he was aware of the soles of his feet pressing on the sunburned earth of Africa. It was a primal quickening that shocked him by its violence. He had never suspected that such a response lay dormant in him, waiting to leap out at the first sniff of the scent of Africa. He felt weak with the swiftness with which his being opened to the dry brilliant air, the smell of the dust that blew from a silent empty continent, the colossal sky, the clear direct way the sun burned over it all. He felt stunned by the impact of the primordial element so violently perceived.

As he stood there, his feet on the hot baked surface of Africa, Europe seemed small, wizened, stale with the weight of its crowded past, dense with its history of successive civilizations.

He drank coffee in the airport lounge and went back to his seat on the plane, still vibrating with the intensity of his response to the grandeur, the unconscious wildness, the purity of the great continent.

They took off again. Breakfast was served. The shock of recognition had jolted the London winter, drizzle, dark streets, out of his system. Soon there were the flat, red-roofed houses set among trees; small rivers meandering over rocky beds; dry stretches of veld dotted with thorn-bushes. The roads seemed shallowly scratched on the earth's crust; the houses, villages, native huts had a look of impermanence about them, an air of unconscious acknowledgment that nature still held the upper hand.

Soon there were the yellow slag heaps of the Johannesburg gold mines; the city spread like a rash along the reef where gold had first been discovered.

The plane landed at Jan Smuts Airport.

10

He was afraid again when he went through Immigration. The Afrikaans accents of the officials immediately caught him in the grip of the seventy-one days.

If the official had any idea of who he was, or the circumstances of his visit, he did not show it. He stamped his visa, presented him with a form to be completed and returned on his departure, and wished him a good stay.

Outside, in the sunshine, Barney and Una waited. Hardly changed after ten years. Their faces a little lined from the ever-blazing sunshine, the red of Barney's hair somewhat faded, Una's amplitude increased by the birth of two more young.

But all the impressions of his arrival receded under the benevolence of the sunshine. He had forgotten the quality of the dry highveld summer. It enfolded him, blessed him. Intrinsic in it was the nature of everything benign he had ever experienced. Everything good, pleasurable, kindly, benefi-cent, conferred without judgment, without cost, was contained in the steady radiance of the summer blaze. It was its own justification. It existed gloriously in its own right.

Barney and Una seemed quite unaware of it. He supposed one must be deprived of it, starved of it for a decade, to acknowledge it as the miracle it was.

In the car, their customary vitality and exuberance were overcast by their awareness of his father's illness. They were unnaturally restrained, as they had been the last time he had seen them. He began to feel again as if he were leprous.

The streets of Johannesburg were unchanged. He could have been a small boy going to nursery school, a youth on his way to a music lesson, a medical student off to classes, a doctor on his way to work. It was just as it always had been. The dazzling sunshine lay over the streets, gardens, hedges; lawns and flower beds flourished. Black nannies pushed white children in prams through the streets. Black men making deliveries for the grocer, butcher, greengrocer, rode along with laden bicycles, whistling, shouting exuberant remarks to passing Africans, flirting with nursemaids.

Amazed, he said, "Everything looks exactly the same. I suppose that because my life has changed I expect everything else to be different too."

Barney said, mournfully, "Oh, it might look the same, old chap," and then tailed off.

Nevertheless, for the first twenty-four hours of his visit he was beguiled by the appearance of sameness. Rosie, waiting in the doorway, overjoyed to see him. Father, sitting up in bed, calm and self-contained. He had always been a spare, lean mean; the only change in him was a look of frailty, so that the fineness of his bone structure was more evident. The starched hospital nurse bustling about the house was a foreign element. Even so, his return had the quality of fitting again into the familiar hollow of one's own mattress, so that habitual patterns are assumed without conscious recollection.

The nurse told him, "Your father has rallied since he heard you were coming." She allowed him to have lunch in the sickroom. Rosie served him a yellow wedge of pawpaw spiked with lemon, cold curried *kingklip* with her homemade

58

bread, granadilla ice cream, dishes she knew he enjoyed and were not available in London. His taste buds awoke and remembered.

His father took in all the news—Margot, the children, his work at the hospital—like some revivifying draft. Last year he had not been well enough to make his annual visit to London, this year he could not move from his bed. There was a lot for him to hear.

He said, "My God, Paul, I'm glad those scoundrels in Pretoria gave you permission to come and see me. I feel much better already."

The first night at home, before he went to bed, he wandered about the house savoring the familiarity of patterns, fixed, deep-rooted, touching recognized objects. His mother had had a good eye, excellent taste, the rooms gave pleasure to body and spirit. Thin old Persian rugs silky on polished wood floors. Antique copper dairy measures that Rosie still kept filled with a profusion of cut flowers from the garden. African wood carvings. Mellow Cape Dutch furniture. Paintings everywhere, by his mother and other South African artists.

In his father's study he turned on the light, and Margot looked down at him from the wall. A portrait done by his mother more than twenty years ago. She had caught Margot's cool look, the pale skin, the large dark eyes that would have been tragic if not for the awareness of irony in the whole set of her expression. The neat intelligent head with its helmet of glossy hair. Somehow, subtly, his mother had managed to convey an idea of reserve informed by will and integrity. She had been devoted to her daughter-in-law.

He slept in his old bedroom. So much spiritual energy expended in the twelve-hour plane journey, in the preceding week grappling with the formidable South African bureaucracy, his body demanded a respite. He slept deeply, dreamlessly, like an untroubled boy.

II

His father rested in the afternoon. He lay in the sun beside the pool in a swimming suit that Rosie had unearthed for him. The heat and the dense blue of the sky seemed the only reality. Margot, the children, the house where they used to live, did not, in this present, exist.

Barney and Una came to visit. "Just look at that white Englishman," Barney said. "I never knew that underneath it all you were that color, old man."

"You'll find you're the same color if you keep out of the sun for ten years. Is there any chance of it, Barney?"

"Chance of what?"

"Getting away from the glorious sunshine of the republic long enough for your suntan to fade."

"Not really, old chap. They've taken away my passport."

"I believe there's something called an exit permit."

Una said, "That's right, Paul, you tell him. Tell him."

She was sewing brightly colored paper flowers on a yellow leotard that her youngest was to wear as one of Titania's fairies in a school production of *A Midsummer Night's Dream*. "He won't listen to me. One day they'll come and take him, and there'll be five fatherless kids." She tore off a thread savagely with her teeth. "Last year a bomb was thrown at our house. A few months ago someone tried to set our car on fire. We can still get out with an exit permit, but this patriotic South African over here refuses to budge."

"What are you waiting for, Barney?"

"It's not all that simple, Paul. I can rationalize on a number of levels. First of all, what could I do in England? I only know Roman Dutch law, so I couldn't practice there. I can't go back to school at my age. Second of all, and I know it's a drop in the ocean, I'm one of the few chaps left here who's prepared to take on political and civil rights cases."

"What do you mean, drop in the ocean!" Una was indignant. "He saved those twenty-one South-West Africans from hanging last year."

"Hey! Whose side are you on, Una my angel?"

"We read all about it in London. You're quite a hero there, Barney. But if they put you in jail, you won't be much use to anyone."

"They won't put me in jail, old man. I'm their show lawyer so they can claim there is still a semblance of judicial process when the U.N. or the International Bar Association starts to squeal."

Una said darkly, "And what when it doesn't suit them any longer?"

Barney said, "Oh Christ, this is such a beautiful bloody place to have to leave. I mean—just look at it, Paul."

He looked at it. His father's two acres of garden. The lawn like velvet being mowed by a black gardener. Herbaceous borders brilliant with scent and color. Shrubs, trees, varieties of English roses flourishing in the southern transplantation. The swimming pool set in a flagstoned terrace. The sky's blue mass, cloudless. Everything shimmering in the dry pure sunlight of six thousand feet above sea level. He knew that around five in the afternoon there would be a quick, refreshing thunderstorm, the earth would drink up the rain gratefully, everything would be washed, fresh, the English roses as gracious as if they prospered in an English garden.

Rosie came out of the house with a tea tray and set the tea things on a table under the great umbrella of a jacaranda tree whose every limb he had climbed as a boy. The tea cloth and napkins were embroidered in cross-stitch. There were scones with cream and homemade fig jam, yeast buns bursting with raisins, butter cake with a lemon icing.

"Look at it, Paul. Such a beautiful bloody country to have to leave. I think I'd shrivel up and die in all that London gloom and fog. And we'd be poor there. They won't allow me to take any of my money out." He bit into a scone that left a rim of whipped cream around his lips. He drank hugely from a small china teacup and held it out to Una to be refilled. "It's tough for a chap to know what to do."

Una said, "So stay. And even if they don't throw you in jail, which they will sooner or later, our kids will leave us one by one. Benny's already in New York. Tess plans to go to university in England. We'll be left with all our money and all our sunshine and an empty house." Her broad lap was filled with small paper flowers—purple, yellow, orange. "If we've been over this once, we've been over it a thousand times."

They drank their tea. Doves murmured in the trees, a rhythmic, comforting cooing.

"I promised Margot I'd try to see Dorothy and Max. Have you got their phone number?"

Una spilled some paper flowers and bent down to retrieve them. Barney placed his teacup on the table and elaborately patted his mouth with the napkin that looked so dainty in his hefty paw. He said, "You can forget about that, old chap."

"Why? They're both out of jail, aren't they?"

"Yes, they're out. He did three years, she did two. The thing is, old man, they're both banned and under house arrest."

At precisely this moment the illusion of "being home" popped like an absurd bubble. He heard the sound of the murmuring doves as an inane racket. He began to feel a little sick from all the sweet things he had eaten for tea. The English-style country house and garden, the Georgian silver tea service and fine bone china, in the relentless glare of the South African sun, began to appear fake, spurious, a one-dimensional scenario plunked onto the African veld, on foundations scraped shallowly out of the baked earth—without a past, or a future. The suffocation of the prison and the airplane began to tighten around him again.

Barney said, "That's how it is with Max and Dorothy. Under house arrest, which means that from sundown to sunrise they are required by law to remain in the house. No visitors at all permitted. They are allowed to go to work every day, and they do see people then. But I wouldn't advise you to try and see them at work. I don't know if you're being watched, but it might land them in trouble. The banning, of course, is an additional exquisite turn of the screw. It means they're not allowed to attend any gathering with a common purpose, so that takes care of their social life for them. Christ man, they can't even play a game of bridge because that's gathering for a common purpose."

Una stitched away industriously at her paper flowers. She said, "One of Barney's banned clients was prosecuted for sitting in the kitchen while there was a party going on in the living room. And last year, Dorothy forgot to report at her local police station. She's supposed to report once a week, but it was the twins' birthday and they were having a little party, just themselves and the kids. Anyway, she got a year's suspended sentence for that little oversight. Suspended except for four days. She went to jail for four days."

Barney said, "Oh, they're efficient. You have to hand it to them. The most goddam efficient police state that's ever existed."

Rosie came out to collect the tea things. Barney congratulated her on the excellence of her baking, and she beamed with pleasure. Standing with the laden tea tray in her hands, she told them, "Auw, I remember when the Madam was alive, we used to have such big parties, and every afternoon there was someone for tea." She shook her head sorrowfully. "Nowadays, there is no one to bake for."

As she walked away over the lawn with her load, he thought, poor old woman, you've had no life of your own, just partaken of ours; when Dad dies all this will be taken away from you too.

Barney said, "Bad as things are, the black political prisoners are much worse off." In the mauve shade, under the gnarled old jacaranda tree, he spoke in a dull voice, his usually sanguine features pale, his round moon face pendulous, jowly. "The Terrorism Act is so vicious and it gives them unlimited powers. They can grab anyone, for any political act, detain them indefinitely without charge or trial, there's no habeas corpus. They dehumanize and depersonalize them with prolonged solitary confinement, then if they still haven't broken them down they torture them. All the old Nazi techniques, plus a few of their own variations. Listen to this one, old man. They conduct interrogations with the prisoner balancing, barefoot, on a couple of bricks, holding another brick high above the head. Then they start firing the questions. If the detainee, not prisoner mark you—George Orwell would have loved that term—if the detainee lowers his arms or loses his balance, he gets beaten with a rubber stick. They keep the interrogation going for twenty-four, forty-eight hours. If the chap starts to fall asleep, they pinch and kick him. They're deprived of water, not allowed to go to the lav so they pee in their pants. Finally, they're so confused by sleeplessness and terror and deprivation that they confess to anything, sign anything. Some of them die under interrogation, of natural causes, the reports always say. There was that charming, chilling little report I read—the Minister of Justice replying to a question in Parliament. It went: a person, identity unknown, date of detention unknown, died while being held. Cause of death, suicide."

Una held out her handiwork and surveyed it, a small

vivid yellow leotard covered with multicolored paper flowers. Head on one side, she considered for a few moments then started stitching again. She said, "And they're clever too. So much goes on that no one ever hears about. Then occasionally there's a leak and we get a glimpse of some of the ghastly things they're doing."

"There's an occasional leak," Barney said, "and a small scandal, a few questions asked in Parliament, a paragraph in the *London Times* and *The New York Times*, and then it all fizzles out. Like the resettlement of Africans in the so-called Homelands. It's a deliberate policy to reduce the urban black population. They force all nonproductive Bantu, as they call them, to leave the urban area where they've always lived. These superfluous Bantu, of course, are the old, the unfit, widows, women with dependent kids, stray kids, and they are forcibly uprooted and shoved off into depressed reserves. On one particularly charming occasion, the schoolchildren were all sent home to tell their parents to start packing, and then the whole community was carted off. The areas where they're dumped are barren, infertile, miles away from anywhere. So any able men in the group have to leave to find work elsewhere. They often deposit a whole community in the bare veld with a few sacks of mealie meal and some tents, no toilet facilities, no running water, nothing. And even where they build houses for them, and provide rudimentary social services, there's just no work for anyone to do in the middle of the *bundu*, so they starve anyway. Jesus, it makes my blood boil just to talk about it, and yet there's no way to stop the bastards." He took out one of his foul-smelling cigars, lit up, and puffed out angry clouds of smoke.

Una said, stitching away as if she were at a ladies' sewing circle, "The Black Sash and the Interchurch Aid Committee have set up soup kitchens and do what they can to help in some of the resettlement areas; one of our more whimsical M.P.'s made a speech in Parliament about the comical aspect of priests in their long black and white dresses trying to pitch tents. He called them a pathetic example of the white villains who come from outside to incite the Bantu. He also insisted that the removals were voluntary and humanely carried out." She shrugged her plump shoulders. "What can you do?"

Barney said, "You're right, old man. I don't know why we stay. Who am I kidding? You should see how we conduct ourselves in court, the legal decorum, the propriety. We go through all the motions of judicial process. It's like a play set up with a prepared script. It's a farce. It could be by Lewis Carroll except for the formidable atmosphere. At important trials there are uniformed police, some with submachine guns, surrounding the court, police dogs, the big boys of the S.B. strutting around."

Una sat, her needle in one hand, a small purple flower in the other, mouth slightly open, listening to her husband.

"I don't know why I even join in their charade. The most we can accomplish is to expose the worst of the police irregularities. Christ, man, even the decent judges are powerless."

Una said, "What's happened to you, Barney? I've never heard you talk like this before, sound so hopeless."

Barney mopped his broad forehead with his handkerchief. He laughed, abashed. "It's having someone to talk to for a change, I suppose. We don't get to see many people these days, you know, Paul. Most of our good friends are gone, or under house arrest. And people, decent people, are afraid to socialize with us. And who can blame them? Our phone is tapped, our house is watched, they take down the registration numbers of cars that come to our place. So. It's really good to be able to talk to an old friend once in a while and blow off some steam."

He stood up. "We'd better be making tracks, Una old girl. Give my best to your Pa, Paul. And if you can get away for a while, come and have dinner one night."

Una gathered up the paper flowers from her lap and shoved everything into a brown paper bag.

They strolled over the lawn to the driveway. The gardener whistled a half-remembered tribal chant as he pushed the mower along, fountains of cut grass spurting up as he worked.

66

Barney opened up the hood of the Mercedes and inspected something in the engine. Through the window Una said, "Oh Jesus, Paul, I wish you'd convince him that we have to leave this miserable country. Did you see his face? I've never seen him like that before, as if he was in agony."

The very beauty of the summer afternoon had an evil aspect, as if, after all he had heard, the landscape ought to turn bleak, desolate. He squeezed Una's cushioned hand.

Barney slammed the hood down and got into the car. "Cheerio, old man."

They drove away.

12

Nurse said, "Your father seems quite chirpy, Doctor," which meant that he could go into the sickroom and visit. In the fresh mornings after breakfast, in the predinner dusk, or late at night if his father could not sleep, they carried on a semicontinuous conversation. Their talk, like the old man's appearance, was pared down to essentials. The strictures laid down by mortality and by the rigors of the police state left little time for trivialities.

Yet there was a tranquility in the times they spent together.

"You know, Paul, I'm not afraid of dying. I've had a full life. Satisfying. I think that when people's lives have been empty, or filled with pain, they find it difficult to face the idea of death, they resent dying. But I've been fortunate, my life has been rich, and now death has a certain logic for me."

The old man spoke, and he listened, trying, as he had on the plane, to locate a center, a pivot of stability within the events which seemed to spin confusingly without meaning about him.

"All my life I've been busy with living. I've had more than the allotted three score and ten. I can't say I would have minded a few more eyars—puttering around in the garden, or knocking a ball around the golf course, or running my clinic. But really, it would be a lack of grace to complain."

"Your mother interested me and fascinated me from the moment I first set eyes on her, until she died. She had vitality. And a fine intelligence, though she was not an intellectual, mind you. Which gave her greater freedom to be her natural, unselfconscious self. Too often intellectuals are either paralyzed, or else their actions arise too narrowly from their reason, and they lack touch with their vital center. Oh, she was in touch with her vital center all right. She was full of vivacity, energy, she had a zest for life. I'm a quiet man, you know, Paul, and she was like yeast, she had that leavening quality. She stirred things up. You could never be dull around her. Even when she was miserable or upset there was a fine flourish about it. She was talented, too. D'you know it's almost impossible to buy one of her paintings these days? The collectors are hanging on to them. And if one does find its way into a private gallery, the price is phenomenal."

"Your mother was an independent woman. She had her life and I had mine. But we needed each other, and if we didn't see as much of each other as some married couples, we always enjoyed each other's company when we were to-gether. Perhaps she should have given more of her time to you, but when she was with you it was always positive and significant and full of excitement. And Rosie was always there as the constant element in your life."

"I sometimes wonder if we should have had more children. But I think that a lot of the creative satisfaction that women derive from having babies, she got from her painting."

69

He mourned, silently, for those unborn brothers and sisters who could have remained with the dying man after his own compassionate leave was over.

"We had a lot of joy from you, though. I'm not complaining. You've always been a satisfying son. I suppose I was a little disappointed when you didn't go into practice with me. I'd always dreamed of our working together and you taking over the practice when I became too doddering. Still, it's probably more stimulating to be an internist than an old-fashioned G.P."

"At the time of your arrest I said to Barney that I wished you had been like the sons of so many of my friends. Good men who go about their business, who do a good job of work but remain uninvolved. But Barney said there are times when, if one doesn't become involved, one cannot consider oneself a good man."

He tried to explain to his father how his involvement had come about, never formally conceived, but consisting of a series of responses to what he simply regarded as duty.

His father said, "Good. I prefer it that way. I am always a little afraid of actions based on ideological foundations. One should cope with the dilemmas as they arise. Life is too complex for simple solutions."

He argued with his father the necessity for establishing one's intellectual and ethical stand in the world so that one knows where one stands in the whole scheme. He said he was lost because he had never figured out his situation, just found himself floundering in the messes he got himself into.

His father was impatient. "Your moral basis manifests itself in what you do, in how you live. Besides, what else is there to morality except acknowledging other people's humanity?

"I suppose I can be criticized for remaining on in a country where the humanity of the majority of the population is denied. But not by me. I've always acknowledged it. I've always treated my black and white patients with the same respect, the same compassion. I treated them all whether they could pay or not. I ran my free clinic in the Township till last year. Where I could be effective I did what I believed was right. Governments rise and fall, but there are always suffering people who need doctors, and that's what I've concerned myself with."

His father's point of view was valid, but it was too simple. The world was more complex and more violent than his father suspected. He had never done more than his father was advocating, yet he had been imprisoned and exiled. One had to search deeper for an answer, but the deeper he looked the more he found himself groping in his own darkness. He could not take the discussion with his father to this level. The old man must die with his set of beliefs intact. They had served him well during his life, and were serving well now as, apparently calmly, he faced his death.

"My father left England in the eighteen-eighties and came to practice medicine here because he had trouble with his lungs and they thought the climate would suit him better. And it did. And the open spaces and the dry sunshine suited his spirit better than the fog and soot of the Midlands. He loved this country. I love it too. I don't see why I should have left because I disapprove of the way they are ruling. It's my country as much as it's theirs. More than it's theirs, the scoundrels, because they are destroying a beautiful land."

He thought about the sudden profoundly affecting knowledge of his own love for the country when he first stepped off the plane, how it had turned into something full of shame and pain in the short time he had been back.

But he could not talk of this to his father either.

13

On an afternoon while his father napped, he took the ancient, well-preserved Bentley and drove to the city to look for presents to take back to his sons. His father's house was in a quiet street that ended in a cul-de-sac. The houses all stood far back in spacious grounds with long driveways leading from the street. The street lay deserted in the sunshine, except for a small black Morris Minor parked at the dead end.

He found his way into town without much difficulty, in spite of the disappearance of old landmarks, in spite of the changes, new parkways, new buildings and skyscrapers that sprang up on every corner of the booming, prosperous city.

He parked the car, and in a gallery that specialized in African art and crafts, he bought an ostrich egg with a pocked porcelain shell for his youngest son, a skin drum, shield, and assegai for the middle one, and for the oldest a mask of highly polished wood, Picassoesque in its reduction to the barest statement of human form.

The streets were crowded. He felt like a foreigner, a tourist in a strange city. The suntanned bare-armed women in sandals and bright dresses, the men in open-necked shirts and light trousers, had the casual sun-dried open look of colonials. There were men in dark business suits who could have been walking on Wall Street or Threadneedle Street, women in the height of fashion who bought their clothes in Paris, London, New York. The Africans, shabby, or in cheap bright clothes, with the exuberance he remembered, talking loudly, laughing, whistling, uninhibited among themselves, their native vitality, in spite of everything, manifesting itself in their native sunshine. On a street corner a tribal woman sat, her hair dressed in hundreds of little clay-covered pigtails, clothed in brilliant colors, beadwork about her forehead, neck, and chest, copper bangles on arms and legs. At her bare black breast she suckled a baby. In a small oasis of tranquillity she ignored the commotion of the traffic and crowds of the newer culture that milled around her. There were black beggars on street corners, blind or crippled, and small black urchins demanding pennies or cigarettes from passersby.

He found himself outside a bookshop he had frequented since his boyhood, and a jab of nostalgia sent him inside. An elderly woman salesclerk, looking no different, as gray and middle-aged as when he was a student, was on a ladder arranging paperbacks on a shelf. She turned round and recognized him. She said, "Hullo, how are you," and went back to her sorting. She knew him, and he realized with a nightmare sense that she had no idea if it was ten days or ten years since he had last been in the shop.

Feeling invisible as he had when he came out of jail, he turned and went out. He made his way back to the car. As he was fumbling with the door key, a voice behind him said, "Doctor." He turned. A black man dressed in khaki shirt and trousers stood there.

"Doctor. You remember me? I used to work at Jan Hofmeyr Hospital. I am Benedict Mashaba, the brother of Abel Mashaba." As he spoke, his face, like a developing film, took on familiarity. He recognized him. They shook hands.

"Of course I remember you. How are you?"

"Oh fine, Doctor, fine."

"Are you still at Jan Hofmeyr?"

"No, I have a job as messenger now at the medical school. As for you, Doctor, how are things with you? I have heard you are living in England these days."

"That's right. I'm home on a short visit. My father is ill."

"I'm sorry to know that. I hope he'll make a speedy recovery." He lowered his voice. "You know about Abel?"

He shook his head.

"He has got life sentence. He is on Robben Island."

Stricken, without appropriate words, he shook his head again.

Benedict went on. "His wife and kids wanted to move to Capetown so it would be easier to visit him, but they would not give her an endorsement to stay in the urban area of Capetown. So she only sees him very seldom when she can get the money for the fare."

"How does she manage?"

"Oh, she has a job. But it is not too easy for her, Doctor. She is still a young woman and she has no husband and the children have no father. I help them a little bit, but I am married now and I have a small boy. But I do what I can, and my wife she understands."

"Things are very bad here."

"Auw, Doctor, you don't know how bad. I mean, we are poor but we have enough to eat, we are not hungry, we have clothes for our backs. But we black people, we cannot trust each other anymore. My own cousins, my good friends, people that I grow up with, I don't know if they are working for the police, they don't know if I am working for the police. I'm telling you, Doctor, we are all afraid, all suspicious of each other. We are all watching each other, we all keep our lips closed. It is a very bad thing when they have made us all distrustful of our own people." He leaned forward, lowering his voice. "How do you think they caught Abel? I'm telling you, Doctor, it was an informer. Auw, it is a shame." He shook his head.

A flick of fear whipped at him. He wanted to get away from this man as quickly as possible. In the same instant he realized how effective their technique was; he was caught in its lash. In his brain he registered the fact that intimidation functioned more effectively than torture because it arrested action at its source. "How long can it go on I wonder."

"It will be a long time, Doctor. All our leaders are in jail or in exile. All our people are afraid. But there are those who are working underground, and our black brothers in free Africa will come to our aid one day when they are strong enough. Perhaps not in my time—perhaps in my little son's time." He shrugged. "But it will come."

"We must hope you are right. Benedict, I would like to give you something to help Abel's wife. Could you get it to her?"

"Of course, Doctor. And I know certainly they would appreciate it."

He had nineteen rand in notes in his pocket. He gave them to Benedict. The profuse gratitude made him feel shabby. He had spent more than that on the mask for his son.

He thought then, what if I am being watched?

He said, "Benedict, I don't know if they're keeping an eye on me. Just in case, perhaps you'd better help me check the front wheel."

As he took some tools from the boot he thought, if he is working for them I am already in too deep to get out.

He handed him a spanner. The black man squatted down beside the curb and removed the hubcap from the front wheel. He tightened all the bolts with the spanner, replaced the hubcap, stood up and kicked the tire a few times as if testing its stability. He grinned, said rather loudly, "I think it will be O.K. now, Doctor."

He said, "Thank you," handed Benedict a coin which he spun in the air and then pocketed, grinning again.

"Good-bye, Doctor."

"Good-bye."

They did not shake hands again. Benedict went off whistling and disappeared among the crowds.

Driving back, he felt sickened. Sickened by the ease and shame of giving money, by the way the encounter was sullied by suspicion, by the fear that he was being followed.

When he turned into the driveway he noticed that the black Morris Minor was no longer there. Ashamed, he thought, one becomes paranoid in this atmosphere.

Before dinner he went upstairs to the study to find a book to read at his solitary meal. A wind had sprung up and the curtains flapped noisily about. As he closed the window, he noticed the small black Morris Minor parked at the dead end at the bottom of the road.

14

After breakfast Nurse bustled in, her starched uniform creaking. She said, "Father isn't feeling so chirpy this morning, Doctor. Perhaps you had better keep it short and sweet."

Long familiar with the tyranny of nursing sisters, he submitted. "All right, Sister, I promise not to stay long."

His father looked drawn, his lips blue. He smiled at his visitor but did not sit up.

He sat down beside him on the bed.

His father said, "The old ticker isn't doing its job too well this morning."

The sunshine poured prodigally into the room, spilled over the Bokhara rug, lit up a copper jug filled with apricot roses.

His father said, "Did you ever see such roses." The air was heavy with their scent. He said, "I've been thinking, Paul. When you leave, why don't you take that portrait of Margot in the study? It's one of the best things Mother ever did." He was short of breath and his voice was low. "Many times people wanted to buy it, but she would never part with it. It will look good in Hampstead, over the fireplace in the sitting room."

"We'd love to have it, Dad. Thanks." He pressed the hand that lay on the blanket.

They were silent for a while in the sunshine and the scent of roses. His father said, "Paul, what was the name of that girl, that lovely Indian girl who was your house physician at Jan Hofmeyr?"

He waited before answering, waited, expecting the petals to rain down off all the roses. The black geometrical design seemed to slide about on the dark red background of the Bokhara rug.

He said, "Zainab Vaswami."

"That's right. Dr. Vaswami. Lovely girl. She helped at my clinic for a while." He spoke slowly, pausing between sentences. "I suppose Barney told you her husband is in jail."

"No."

"Some trumped-up charge. Of course they wanted him out of the way. He's a first-rate lawyer. Made all sorts of difficulties for them over the Group Areas Act when they started pushing all those poor Indian families out of their homes and their businesses. He never could stop them, of course, but he did obstruct their high-handed methods for a while. They gave him four years."

"Four years." Four years. Zainab. First me. Then Ahmed. Now her husband. They have taken all her men away from her.

His father said, "By now he must have done at least half his sentence. She's got two little boys, I believe. She's a fine woman—keeps going very well. She's got a flourishing practice in Minto Street in Fordsburg."

Sister hustled in. "Ting-a-ling. Playtime's over. Time to rest now, Doctor dear. Dr. Fielding will be here for your checkup after lunch, and we don't want him scolding me for not taking proper care of you, do we now?"

He took his copy of the *British Medical Journal*, went out into the garden, and sat down on a bench. He tried to read. He was still in the middle of the same article he had been reading in front of the fire last week in London when the telephone call had come through from Johannesburg. He read a paragraph three times, getting no meaning from it. He looked at the pool, but had no heart for swimming or sunbathing. As the sun moved toward the zenith, the heat almost had substance, as though one would be buoyant in it. It blazed with dry, steady radiance, pure in the high altitude of the city.

Restless, he looked around the garden, recognizing every detail. The rockery filled with the cushioned colors of flowering succulents, where he had once fallen and cut his forehead open. He ran his finger over the scar where his father had stitched the wound almost forty years ago. The swing, hanging from a stout bough in the oak tree, on which Rosie had pushed him when he was little; later he had learned to propel himself so that his feet reached into the leaves at the end of the arc he swung through. His own sons used to swing on it when they visited their grandfather, but had gone away before they grew old enough to acquire such proficiency.

Things that had taken place in that garden years ago seemed as vivid and palpable as the scar on his forehead. What was happening in the present had the quality of a dream, a bad dream from which one struggles helplessly to wake.

His eyes were drawn beyond the oak tree. The syringa tree had grown large, its trunk had broadened, its limbs gnarled and thickened. It was in full flower, hung with grapelike bunches of starry lavender flowers.

He sat on, slumped on the garden bench, his journal unread beside him, contemplating the syringa, perceiving its scent of spice and musk without needing to go over to sniff the fleshy blooms.

Rosie came out to ask if he would like his lunch served

outdoors. He said he would come in. She grumbled at him, "Why are you just sitting outside with all your clothes on, Paulie—you should be swimming and enjoying the summer. You are going back to such a terrible cold climate."

After lunch Eugene Fielding came. A most eminent physician. They had been at medical school together. They shook hands. "Paul, it's good to see you. Sorry it's such sad circumstances that bring you home. How are Margot and the boys?"

Like the others, Eugene looked much the same, suntanned, face a bit dried out by constant exposure to the sun.

"You're father's a terrific old man, Paul. A wonderful patient. He knows exactly what the score is, he's calm and intelligent about it, he submits unquestioningly to all the treatment I prescribe."

"What exactly is the situation, Eugene?"

"Well, he's in intractable failure, Paul. He was responding to the digitalis and diuretics quite satisfactorily for a while, but not anymore. That's why I thought it was time to send for you. He's decompensating, breathless, can't really get about anymore. I'll go and take a look at him. Sister tells me he's a little better since you got here."

He hung about in the cool, dim hall, waiting for Eugene. He felt chilly, went through the french windows of the sitting room out onto the terrace. White-painted garden furniture stood about, arranged as it was in his mother's day, the round metal table under a bright fringed umbrella, huge clay pots filled with cascading ivy geraniums, a bronze abstract sculpture, well weathered, by Magarshak, who came regularly for years to Mother's Sunday afternoon outdoor salon. During the war, the house was a haven to droves of refugee European artists. Mother's taste and eye everywhere evident in the almost Mediterranean look of the terrace, the bougainvillaea spilling purple over the whitewashed wall in the hot afternoon. Father dying inside the cool house. Eugene listening to his faltering heart, measuring his falling blood pressure. Margot and the children thousands of miles away in the chill of an English February. At the back of the mind an idea that some sense should be accessible to him out of all this chaos, if he had not the continuous sensation of floundering about in his own darkness.

Eugene joined him on the terrace. "He's going to have a nap now. I left Sister tucking him in. She's a darn good nurse, that woman. I'm afraid he can't hold out for too long now, Paul. His blood pressure is only ninety over fifty, his heart's grossly irregular. It will be a matter of days, a week perhaps. I presume you'll stay to the end."

He shook his head, feeling like a leper again, the strictures placed on him excluding him from normal society, making him a recipient of people's pity and horror. "I have to leave on Saturday. They've only let me in for one week."

"One week." Eugene paled, looked deeply shocked.

He thought, he's had no contact with the police state, yet here it is, casting its barred shadow over this sunny terrace, over both of us. In the uncomfortable silence, he felt a wave of pity for his friend. He knew Eugene, a physician with talent and integrity, would have functioned with the same compassion and excellence wherever he lived; from the day he had first entered medical school, medicine had been his only concern, his passion. He was cut off from all the other aspects of South African life. Even his wife and children were second to his patients. His family were quiet and mousy and devoted to him; he ate warmed-up food that dried out waiting for him in ovens; he left his bed, dinner parties, theatres, uncomplainingly when his patients needed him. Now, out on this charming terrace, some sinister extraneous element was impinging on his narrow awareness, and he was discomfited and shamed and without adequate means to respond.

He felt a need to comfort Eugene. He thought, we are both of us diminished by the degradation of this thing. He said, "Well, at least they've let me come and see him. Even if it's only a week, it's better than nothing."

Rosie came out with a tray with glasses and a jug in which ice and lemon slices and mint leaves tumbled about.

"Dr. Eugene loves my lemon squash," she announced. "He always drinks some when he comes to see the old master."

"I've been asking her for the recipe for years," Eugene said, "but she won't part with it."

"You can always drink it whenever you come here," Rosie told him.

They sat under the gay umbrella, drinking, their humiliation only partially dispelled by Rosie's hospitality.

Eugene finished two glasses of lemon squash. He said, "I'm sure she sweetens it with honey." He stood up. "I must get a move on now, Paul; I'll look in again tomorrow."

"Are you going back to your consulting rooms now, Eugene?"

"Yes."

In an instant he found himself propelled into a course of action he had not for one conscious moment contemplated. Yet later that night, when he looked back on how he had spent the afternoon, it occurred to him that he had behaved as if every single step had been meticulously planned beforehand.

He said, "Eugene, could you give me a lift into town?"

"With pleasure."

He ran upstairs to his bedroom to put on his jacket and tie. He looked out of the window that faced the street and saw the black Morris Minor parked in the cul-de-sac, a man at the wheel reading a newspaper. He took from the bureau a handful of money, loose change, which he held in his fist as he went downstairs. At the hall telephone, he hurriedly skimmed through the directory, located an address. He stuck his head into the kitchen, told Rosie he was going into town with Eugene and would be back before dinner.

He rejoined Eugene on the terrace, and they strolled off to the car. The driveway curved from the street past the back of the house and widened into a parking area at the side entrance. Here Eugene had left his car. They both got in. As the engine started up he felt his blood racing, his mouth dry. Eugene released the footbrake, slid into first gear.

As the car started to pull away, he opened his fist and

dropped the handful of money over the floor. Eugene braked. He apologized for his carelessness.

"Let me help you pick it up."

"Don't bother, thanks Eugene. Just drive on, I'll pick it up as we go." He bent over, doubled up, and started collecting the spilled coins. When he lifted his head again they had turned the corner and were two blocks away from the house. He turned and looked out of the rearview window. Behind them was a chauffeur-driven gray Cadillac and a black milkman on his delivery bike. Beyond that, the road was empty.

He leaned back in his seat. For the rest of the journey he kept the conversation to his work at the hospital in London in an effort to mitigate Eugene's evident helplessness in a situation where the good man found himself without armor or ammunition, where his narrow dedication left him without resources in any field but his own.

15

The consulting rooms were in an impressive skyscraper of concrete and plate glass. He went with Eugene as far as the lobby to admire the shallow pool with its fountain and tropical fish, its mosaic mural depicting the rise and development of the gold-mining industry. He declined an invitation to go up with the fabricated excuse that he had to look for gifts to take back to the boys.

He walked across the town through the unfamiliar familiar streets. He passed the main branch of the public library where, as a boy, he had gone every Saturday morning to change his books. He headed away from the commercial European area of the city, walked past the municipal market where small African boys staggered by under the loads of fruit and vegetables they carried to the cars of white housewives.

Beyond the market the town thinned out into warehouses and small industrial plants, the sidewalks became narrower and littered with garbage. He passed a bicycle shop from which the plaintive notes of penny-whistle jazz emerged jauntily, catching at his heart.

Fewer and fewer white faces, less traffic, small shops, shabby houses, and blocks of flats. He was in the Indian quarter of the town. It looked shabbier and more poverty-stricken than he remembered. He knew the area was smaller now as thousands of Indians had been cleared out of their homes and businesses to make space for white-owned industry and commerce. The sun's glare which enhanced his father's garden, here exposed without mercy the meanness, the filth, the cheap tawdriness of the goods in the shopwindows. Indian children played about on the pavements, little girls with long heavy plaits of dark hair, gold earrings in pierced ears; little boys in short serge knickers and English-schoolboy knee socks and shoes. Women in saris sat in the shade of their *stoeps*, moved in and out of the shops.

A huge black car drove slowly along the street, a gleaming brand-new Buick, filled with what appeared to be several generations of an Indian family. He remembered as a small boy asking his mother why so many Indians possessed such magnificent cars and her explaining that, as they were only allowed to own small houses in a slummy section of the town, wealthy Indians could indulge in little luxury other than expensive cars. Now, he thought, they are even being driven out of their slums.

A few familiar landmarks were no longer where he looked for them, and he was not sure if he could find his way. Turning a corner, he looked about to try and get his bearings. Across the road was a low block of flats, pink paint peeling from the stuccoed surface, the window frames painted turquoise. He counted three windows up and two to the left. There was the window. Bare now. Behind the drawn curtains the late afternoon sun had filtered onto the bed, onto Zainab's limbs and his, two bodies, one brown, one pale, languorous on the bed, her black hair loosed luxuriant over the pillows. Her scent of syringa. The intensity of the westerly sun paling into dusk as they lay together. The only time they had had to make love was that unused portion of the day, after work, before dinner. Dr. Vaswami, divested of starched hospital coat, of silken sari.

Encountering Indian women in London occasionally, he would relish the idea of divulging to them his expertise at the intricacies of tucking, pleating, draping a sari.

If he stood at the corner any longer staring up at the window of Zainab's old flat he would attract attention. He pulled himself away. He walked on, amazed again at the vividness of the past, the tenuousness of the present.

Two small Indian girls were turning a skipping rope for a third who jumped up and down, her sari bunched in her fists, exposing thin brown legs in white ankle socks and black school shoes. He asked the tallest if she knew where Minto Street was. She stopped turning the rope, turned her head, giggled into the palm of her hand. The two friends gazed at him with flat black eyes.

A horse and cart clip-clopped along the road, an Indian "Sammy," vendor of fruit and vegetables, who gave him the directions he needed.

He reached a block of small shops and offices. Halfway along the block he stopped at a door with a polished brass plate on it. Dr. Zainab Vaswami. M.B.B.Ch. D.C.M. His heart tripped. He moved on. Next door was the office of an Indian attorney. Then a draper's store, a tailor, a confectioner's shop, its window piled with a mass of vivid pink and green and yellow sweetmeats and syrupy cakes.

He chose the draper's store. It was small, crowded with Indian customers. A young shop assistant came forward. He asked to see some saris. The young man looked unsure, said he would get his father and disappeared through a door. Two small boys were squatting in the doorway playing with marbles. The older looked about ten.

He approached them. "Do you know where Dr. Vaswami's office is?" Yes, yes, the older one replied, he knew it well, it was only two doors away, he could take him there at once. He stood up, abandoning his marbles.

"Could you just take a note there for me?"

The boy was willing, eager.

He saw an invoice lying discarded on the floor. He picked it up; Patel Bros. Drapers. Minto St. Fordsburg. Jhb. The back of it was grubby but blank. He took a pen from his pocket and wrote: Zainab, can you see me? I am in Patel's shop next door. Paul.

He folded it, said to the boy, "After you've given this to her, come back here and I'll give you some money to buy sweets. Give it to the doctor, no one else."

The boy ran off. An elderly Indian man appeared behind the counter. "What sort of saris would you like to see, sir? I have large selection, pure silk, cotton, lawn, nylon, assorted colors, very fine quality." He pulled open a drawer, heaped a pile of brilliant fabrics on the counter. "Now look at this one, sir, did you ever see such workmanship? Look at the embroidery, all done by hand I assure you. I import them myself from Bombay. This yellow one, first quality one hundred percent pure silk. The embroidery is worked in real silver thread. Feel it, sir, just feel the softness, see how it drapes."

He held it up to show how it spilled in supple folds. "This red one with gold embroidery I assure you, sir, it is genuine gold. It is not cheap but for such workmanship one must expect to pay a price." He turned around for a further selection.

At his shoulder a low voice said, "Paul. It *is* you. I thought I was dreaming."

He turned his head, saw Zainab's black hair drawn into a glistening knot at the nape of her neck. Saw a small fine ear pierced with a gold earring, the smooth dark honey cheek, the curve of cheekbone and brow forming the setting for the large brilliant eye. He smelled syringa.

His jacket was tugged roughly. Behind him the small boy was demanding payment. He gave him twenty cents and the boy darted off out of the shop.

The shopkeeper was speaking. "How are you, Dr. Vaswami? My grandson is very much better since my daughter-in-law brought him to see you. He is not coughing such a lot now. What can I do for you today, Doctor?"

Zainab said, "I need some handkerchiefs, Mr. Patel."

"If you don't mind I will tell my son to help you. I am showing this gentleman saris."

He said, "I can wait. I'm not in a hurry. I'll try and make up my mind meanwhile."

The shopkeeper went off. He turned, looked at her.

"Zainab."

"Paul. Why are you here?"

"My father is dying. They've let me come to see him. One week. I leave on Saturday. Zainab. It's a feast for me just to look at you."

She touched her cheek with the back of her hand. "I've gone old. It is such a long time, Paul."

He saw that her beauty was not only unblemished, but had intensified. The roundness, softness, that had gone from cheek and chin, revealed the sculptured quality of the facial bones. The beauty of the girl was distilled in the woman, purer, stronger. The only sign of the strain of the years was the dark smudges under the eyes.

"You are more beautiful that ever. I couldn't leave without seeing you. I think I am being watched." Her eyes widened. "I was afraid to try to get in touch with you. I didn't know if it was safe to phone. I managed to give them the slip this afternoon, but I didn't want to take any chances."

Mr. Patel placed a pile of boxes of handkerchiefs in front of Zainab. Lacy, embroidered, exquisite.

"Oh no, Mr. Patel. I just want some plain white cotton hankies."

He took them away.

He said, "Zainab. My father told me this morning about your husband."

The heavy lids lowered over her eyes, the lashes casting shadows on her cheeks. He asked, "How is he, Zainab?"

"He is coping very well. It is more than two years already, more than half over. The hardest part is done, it will go quickly now."

"His spirit?"

She looked up. "Very good. He is studying for a degree in philosophy." She smiled.

In a room at the back of the shop a child wailed and a woman's voice began to scold loudly. Mr. Patel excused himself and disappeared behind the door.

"Your children, tell me about them."

"Two boys. Seven and four. We all live with my parents. We manage well. I have a very busy practice."

"And you, Zainab?"

The repose on her face he remembered, as though she had some source of stillness on which she could draw, some well of quietness that calmed and restored her.

"I am too busy to think much, Paul."

"How about these, Dr. Vaswami, finest Irish lawn, hand-rolled edges."

"Thank you, Mr. Patel. Give me half a dozen, please."

He went off to wrap them.

"When your husband comes out—leave this place, Zainab. Come to London. I can always help you get a job."

"Paul, don't you remember how I loathed London when I was studying for my diploma? All those poor Indian women shivering in their thin saris with thick boots and heavy coats. And the smell of cabbage, and the rain. Besides, they're not letting Indians into England these days; they have taken a leaf from South Africa's book."

He stood, silent. She lifted a length of purple silk sari that lay on the counter, let it slip through her fingers. "Ismael will never leave this country no matter how often they arrest him. It is our country." She shrugged. "We have nowhere else to go."

Mr. Patel brought Zainab her package. "We will charge it to your account, Doctor, with a special discount for you, of course."

The parcel in her hand dangling from a string loop, she looked unsure what to do next. He said, "I wonder if you would be kind enough to help me choose a sari for my wife. I'm not very good at shopping."

She said, "Of course." She spoke to Mr. Patel in

Gujerati, and he went away to the back of the shop. "I told him to take away this rubbish and show you something decent." She smiled, shook her head, "I have a waiting room crowded with patients."

He felt a landslide of time rumbling away downhill taking him, helpless, along with it. He said, "Zainab. Just one thing. I must know. Do you—those years we were together—do you regret them? Did I cause you much pain?"

She reflected, head bowed, her fingers, scrubbed, with short-clipped nails, ringless, smoothing out the folds in the gossamer stuff of one of the saris. She said, "Yes—it was miserable for me at times, Paul," then, looking at him, added, "but even so—I remember those years with so much pleasure."

In the crowded shop he could not touch her.

He said, "That is what I came to find out."

She said, simply, "Thank you."

Mr. Patel came back with a box of saris. They chose a dark red silk with gold metallic embroidery, a pale blue cotton with white embroidery. While they were being wrapped Zainab said, "He is cheating you gloriously."

"It's a small price to pay for seeing you."

"I simply must go now, Paul."

"Zainab, if you ever need anything, if there's anything at all—"

"I know, Paul. I have always known."

"Just Saint Giles Hospital, London, will get me."

One more look that sought and held him. "I'm sorry about your father, Paul. He's a fine man and a very good doctor. Good-bye." Her pink sari flickered through the crowd and out the door.

Mr. Patel brought him his package and his change. "I am sure your wife will be very well satisfied with these. Very glad to be of service." He accompanied him to the door, well satisfied himself with the transaction.

16

The afternoon sun beat steadily down on the city.
Walking back into town he took off his jacket and carried it
slung over his shoulder. He found his way back to the bus
terminus. He had not used the bus since his student days.

An off-duty bus conductor, sitting on a bench engrossed
in an American comic book, affirmed that the number
twenty-two still ran the same route, that it would, in fact, be
leaving in eight minutes. He sat down to wait on a bench
marked *Whites Only*. The bus came and he climbed up to the
top deck and sat down in the front seat, the package with the
saris beside him. He saw himself, a small boy, every Saturday
morning sitting in this same seat, his violin in its case next to
him, his pile of library books on his lap. He thought
fleetingly of the vulnerable back of the neck of his youngest
son and was pierced through with pity and tenderness.

The conductor came upstairs clicking his ticket puncher.
He told him his destination and found the fare had more than
doubled since his youth. The bus trundled through the
congested city, past the lush damp gardens and lawns of the
Joubert Park, the museum, where his grandmother's beaded

satin wedding dress was displayed in a glass case. Up the hill to Hillbrow, the bus stopping on the corner next to the telephone booth from which he had phoned Una when he was released from jail. Momentarily the terror encapsulated him. He strove to recall the curve of Zainab's cheek, the pink sari across her shoulder as she stood quiet beside him in Patel's shop, and was able to draw on her stillness; to pass with relative calm the prison that skulked square and fortress-like just beyond the medical school. Prison and medical school, he thought, the two institutions of my education standing cheek by jowl.

The bus entered the green of the northern suburbs. From where he sat the layout of the large estates could be seen, swimming pools glistening like blue jewels in almost every garden, the verdant lawns maintained, despite the high dry heat, by vigilant black gardeners and perpetually swirling sprays of water dampening the turf.

He went downstairs, tugged the bellpull. The conductor standing on the platform said, "Not your stop yet, sir." He panicked as if the conductor might restrain him and jumped off before the bus quite came to a halt. Looking back he saw the stationary bus, the conductor staring oddly at him.

He walked quickly away, taking the first turn to the left, into a road the gardens of which abutted on the backs of the houses of the street where his father lived. He turned into the gateposts of the third house from the corner. A semicircular driveway enclosed an arc of immaculate lawn and rockeries that had the look of multicolored waterfalls. The main part of the garden was beyond the whitewashed, Cape Dutch gabled house.

The front door was of heavy studded oak, the doorway overhung by a profuse wistaria creeper heavy with grapelike clusters of pale mauve, scented blossoms. He rang the bell. The door was opened by a black man in an impeccable white uniform with a maroon sash slung over one shoulder.

He said, "Good afternoon, is Mrs. Ellison in?"

The servant let him into the hall. "Wait one moment please, Master." He strode off, more than six feet tall, with magnificent bearing.

He thought, what will I do if they're all out.

A door opened and a woman came into the hall. Middle-aged, blue-rinsed white hair exquisitely coiffed, pearls round her throat, diamonds glinting on fingers and pinned onto the bosom of her pale blue linen dress. For a moment she looked blank, then she said, "Paul!"

"Mrs. Ellison."

She came up to him, put her arms around him, kissed him warmly, smelling fresh and expensive. "Paul. I didn't recognize you for a moment. What a wonderful surprise! We knew you were coming to see Daddy but didn't dream you would spare the time to visit us. Come in, my dear, come in."

She led him into the palatial drawing room; the late afternoon sun flooded the french windows and the terrace beyond which he could see the parklike gardens, the swimming pool, tennis court, the high hedge that separated the property from his father's garden. Two white-clad figures darted about on the tennis court.

"Won't you sit down. My dear Paul. Let me look at you. It's been such a long long time. I'm so sorry about Daddy. Now you must tell me all your news. It's a bit late for tea, so just let me ring for Samson to bring us drinks. What will you have, dear?"

"Whiskey and soda would be fine, thank you."

She rang and the manservant came in. "Whiskey and soda, Samson, and ask Triphena if she's got something nice to go with it." The servant departed silently over the Chinese silk carpet.

He held up his package. "I've been into town to buy some saris for Margot. She likes to make them into dresses. I took the bus back and stupidly got off at the wrong stop, and as I was passing your house I thought I'd stop by to say hullo."

"I'm so very glad you did, Paul." She lowered her voice. "Tell me dear, how *is* Daddy?"

He said, "Not too good."

"Oh my dear, I am devoted to that man. We've been neighbors for forty-five years. I still miss the sight of your dear mother working in the garden in those *marvelous* big

93

floppy hats she used to wear. And I must tell you, Paul," her voice warmed as she drew him into the hearth of her confidence, "that since your father retired we've never really found another doctor. I mean, we occasionally have to call someone in, but it is just not the same thing."

The servant came in wheeling a trolley with glasses, scotch, soda syphon, and a tray of small savory tarts. White-gloved, he served the drinks.

Watching the performance, he wondered in what extravagant fantasy the servant's uniform had been dreamed up, deciding that the red sash, slung over the left shoulder and ending in a silk fringe swinging jaunty at the hip, must be a heritage of the British Raj in India. He thought, no longer an outpost of the British Empire but still holding doggedly on to some of the more quaint imperialist customs.

"Come on, Paul, you must try some of Triphena's cheese and mushroom patties. She's famous for them."

The hot savory pastry melted in his mouth, stuck in his chest. He washed it down with scotch. There was no need to talk. Mrs. Ellison chattered endlessly like a glittering tropical bird. "That's Stephanie out there on the court. She has a group of girls and they play tennis here three times a week. She has her own pool, of course, but she and Donald decided it was a waste to build a court when ours is hardly ever used, so they play here. Did you know she's got five children now, Paul, each one more beautiful than the next? And Daddy's taken Donald into the firm and he's doing very nicely thank you. They go to Europe or the States at least once a year. In fact, we keep a flat in London, just off Baker Street, for the family to use. Here comes Steffy now."

Two women strolled over the lawns, up the shallow steps onto the slate-paved terrace, through the wide open french windows into the drawing room. He stood up.

"Steffy—you'll never guess who's dropped in."

A woman with the trim figure of an athletic schoolgirl removed her sunglasses and looked up at him. Her brief white tennis dress exposed smooth brown arms and thighs, well-muscled calves. Blond hair swung to her shoulders. Under the bronzed skin of her snub pretty face, lines etched by the sun revealed that she was forty rather than fourteen.

"It's Paul," she said. She shook hands, put up her face like a child's to be kissed. "Paul, for God's sake where did you appear from? This is Karen." She introduced the other lithe, slightly wizened athlete in trim white shorts and shirt. "Paul and I went to nursery school together," she explained. "My God, Paul, I hate to think how long ago that was." She explained to her companion, "That's Paul's father's house over there." She waved a brown, ringed and braceleted hand breezily in the direction of the windows. "We grew up practically in each other's laps, didn't we, Paul? Used to play school-school and house-house together. Oh goody, I see we're just in time for drinks, Mummy, and Triphena's made some of those yummy mushroom thingummies."

She flung her racquet onto an antique sofa, filled glasses with scotch and soda for herself and her friend, crammed a patty into her mouth, sprawled in an armchair, legs apart.

He thought, except for the lines round her eyes and mouth, and the fact that she's drinking scotch instead of orange squash, she is unchanged from when she was fourteen.

Mrs. Ellison addressed her daughter in hushed tones. "Steffie, Paul's father is very ill. Paul's specially come all the way from London to see him."

"Oh God—I'm sorry, Paul. I didn't know. Your Dad is an absolute honey." She explained to Karen. "Paul's father vaccinated me, inoculated me, saw me through the mumps, measles, chicken pox, you name it." She licked some flaky crumbs off her fingers.

Karen inquired, "You live in London?"

He nodded.

Stephanie said, "My God—Paul—I envy you. This place is foul. Deadly. Nothing ever happens here. If we want decent clothes or food or just to see a good show, we have to go to London or New York. And the Nat. Government. Honestly, I swear they're getting worse every day. Every time there's a decent book or a movie, they censor it or ban it. Do you know we have to spend half our time when we're in London, chasing movies to see all the juicy bits they cut out over here. Honestly. It's enough to make you puke."

Karen said, "They really are ridiculous."

Mrs. Ellison remarked, "And Daddy's short of skilled labor at the factories and they will not allow him to use natives for the jobs. And the natives are only too willing to take on the skilled work, but no, we're not allowed to employ them."

Stephanie, squirting soda into another scotch, said, "Pa should just use the natives anyway, and to hell with their stupid laws."

"He can't just do that, Steffy. The labor inspectors visit the factories regularly to check up. They tell us that job reservation is for the protection of white skilled workers. So Daddy said to one of them the other day—what white skilled workers, where are they? He was quite frank with the man, he told him—if you fellows won't let me use blacks then for goodness' sake get me some whites, man, I could double my production. Of course the idiot of an inspector said it wasn't his fault, it's the law, and his job is just to see that apartheid functions properly."

Outside he could see two gardeners working in the oblique light of the falling sun. One was skimming leaves off the surface of the pool, the other was rolling up the tennis net. Beyond the hedge at the far end of the estate he could glimpse the red tile roof of his father's house. In the street in front of his father's house, in a small black Morris Minor, an employee of the Special Branch, the secret police, was keeping watch. If he were to mention this fact to the three women with whom he was drinking whiskey, they would be incredulous. They would think he was joking, or lying, or, at most, insane.

The athletic friend was speaking. "So she tells me that her car broke down, and there was this African just standing there, so she said to him—hey, Jim, can you help me—and he just turned around and walked away. So I said, serves you right for calling him Jim. So she asks me—what could I have called him, I didn't know what his darn name was. And I told her quite frankly, I said, why couldn't you just say, excuse

96

me, can you help me, same as you would to a white man?"

He stood up. He asked, very casually, "Is that gap in the hedge still there that Stephanie and I used to go through?"

Mrs. Ellison said, "I'm sure it's still there—it might be a bit overgrown. What a good idea, Paul. It will save walking all the way round the block."

Stephanie said, "Hang on. I'm leaving in a few minutes, Paul, I'll drive you back. If I stay here long enough for one more drink, Nanny will have the monsters bathed and fed by the time I get back. As soon as I walk in they all start carrying on, and they're perfect angels when they're with the nanny."

"Don't bother, thanks, Stephanie. I'll just nip through the hedge."

Mrs. Ellison said doubtfully, "You might get your clothes all dusty."

"It will be quite all right. Thank you so much, it was good to see you."

"Why don't you come over and have dinner, Paul? Don would love to see you, and I'd show you our five repulsive brats."

"I'm sorry, Stephanie, there isn't time, I'm only here for a few days." He kissed the cheeks of the two women, shook hands with the third. Mrs. Ellison said, "Now don't forget to give my love to Daddy and remember me to Margot." He took his package of saris and went out.

At the hedge, he found the gap, much overgrown, almost impassable. He turned and waved to the women who were watching from the terrace. He pushed his way through the woody growth. Dust rose, filled his throat, a branch he pushed aside sprang back and hit him across the forehead. As he emerged on the other side the bottom of his jacket was tugged. In a panic he turned and ripped a branch off its stem, freed himself, shoved the torn limb back in the hedge and hurried over the lawn, past the swing in the oak tree, past the syringa bush, into the house.

He went straight upstairs to his room and looked out the window. The black Morris was still there, the man sitting at the wheel.

17

Nurse came by carrying a tray. "Father ate nearly all his din-dins, Doctor. He seems pretty chirpy tonight."

In his father's room a dim lamp burned. The curtains were wide open to the summer night. There had been a brief heavy shower with thunder and lightning before dinner. The refreshed earthy scent of the wet garden came in at the windows.

"Turn off the lamp, Paul. We'll be able to see the sky. There's a full moon tonight."

In the dark the sky was violet. The lawn sloped damp and silver away from the windows, the trees and shrubs black, without substance. Metallic scales glimmered on the surface of the pool.

"A perfect summer night, eh, Paul? By jove I love the highveld weather. I'm sure this must be the finest climate in the world. And the garden; I think I know every blade of grass, every leaf, the texture of every tree trunk."

"It's a beautiful garden. I sometimes dream about it in London, when it rains all summer and we forget what the sun looks like."

"It's supposed to be one way of keeping the lawns green—take some grass seed and let it rain for a hundred years. We have to keep the sprinklers going all summer."

Doves murmured in their sleep under the eaves.

"Did you have a good day? What did you do this afternoon, Paul?"

It was suddenly as clear to him as the moonlight that his father had sent him to see Zainab today.

He said, "I went to see Zainab Vaswami."

"Did you? Oh good. I hoped you would."

Puzzled, he asked, "Why did you want me to go, Dad?"

"Well, I suppose I'm a tidy man."

In the luminous silence that filled the room there was the sound of a muffled flurry under the eaves, some agitation in the dove's nest.

"You knew about Zainab and me?"

His father nodded.

He was intrigued. "How did you know?"

"Margot told me."

Night sounds came in from the garden, raindrops dripping off leaves, the rhythmic sawing of crickets, frogs crooning around the pool.

He said, "Margot." Then he said, "When?"

"When? When it was happening I suppose."

"Tell me."

"Let me try to remember. It was a long time ago. It was one afternoon, I think I must have been visiting a patient who lived near you. And I dropped in to have tea with Margot and the boys. Yes, that's it. We had tea in the garden. I remember the boys were digging in the sandpit. And Margot told me."

"What did she say?"

"Oh, she said something like, um—Dad, Paul is having a love affair. And I suppose I said, oh, who is it? And she said—you know the beautiful Indian girl, his senior house physician. And I must have said, whew, or something like that."

He waited for his father to go on.

"And then I asked her, do you mind very much, Margot? And she said something that made me respect her. I mean, I've always loved and admired Margot, but for this I respected her." His father paused, took a sip from a glass of whiskey and water that Nurse had left on the bedside table.

Waiting, it seemed his heart stood still.

"She said—yes, I do mind, very much, but, I'm ashamed to say that I don't care whatever Paul does, just as long as he always comes back here, to me. Now I thought that was a wonderfully wise and loving thing for a woman to say. And I told her so. And she said, oh, in a rueful but amused way, you know how she is, Paul, she said that it didn't prevent her from feeling jealous and hurt and all that sort of thing."

He could hear the frogs crooning their mournful song down by the water.

His father said, "She's a strong, gentle woman, Margot, strong enough to love you and let you live, gentle enough to suffer for it."

He asked, "Were you able to comfort her, Dad?"

"I think so. I told her that you surely loved her, and that your relationship with this girl was something apart from your marriage and took nothing from it. She asked me how I could be so sure."

As his father paused for a rest, he could see that he was smiling. He went on. "I told her I could be sure because many years ago I had had a love affair. I said to her, now—you see what sort of family you've married into—and we both laughed."

He asked, "Did you say that to console her?"

"Certainly not!" His father was mildly indignant. "It was the truth."

He moved from his chair and went to the window. His back to the garden, he sat on the sill, facing his father. By a faint change in the atmosphere, a minute shift in perception, they were no longer a middle-aged son and a dying father;

they were two men, brothers perhaps, in the world, communing, acknowledging each other's individualness.

"You were about twelve years old, I suppose. Oh, she was a beautiful girl, beautiful. A sculptress. It was an intoxicating time of my life. I can only recall it with pleasure."

"Did Mother know?"

"Well, she was away in Paris taking a painting class with someone or another when it started. She probably knew. But she had enough sense, and confidence in our marriage, to know that this was something—apart. Most people don't realize this, you know, Paul, and they eat themselves and each other up, and marriages fall apart. I mean, I'm not advocating polygamy. Love in marriage is, I think, a more precious and rare thing. But a love affair has an intensity and a sweetness, even a painfulness, of its own. It's quite unlike anything else. Of course it's ephemeral. Has to be. Its intensity derives from its awareness of its own fragility. But that's all right too. Society would collapse if people were in love all the time."

The dark soft abundance of the summer night filled the room. In the light from the night sky he could see his father smiling, his silver hair showing in the dimness.

"She went back to England, and it was painful for a time. But it's always remained a source of joy to me." He leaned back on the pillows, a little breathless.

He went over to the bed and felt his father's pulse.

"Don't worry, Paul, I'm fine. Just the old heart jumping about a bit at the memory of that delightful time."

He sat down again by the window.

"I'm a fortunate man, Paul. My life has been good."

"It's not only fortune, Dad, it's how you deal with what's—handed to you. And you've always dealt with yours—with grace."

"Well, it's nice of you to say so. Meanwhile, how was it with Dr. Vaswami today?"

He said, "It was very brief. But good."

Creaking and bustling, Nurse came in. She turned on the

lights. "That's enough sitting about in the dark and gossiping for tonight. You must take your medicine now, Doctor dear, and it's time for bye-byes."

He went out of the room disquieted and left uncomfortable by a flitting mirror-image of himself he had caught as the old man reminisced; brooding, ill at ease, by the dim lamplight in the study, he began to see his father and himself now as confederates in the maintenance of the unexamined life, justifying their self-indulgence in a way guaranteed not to injure their self-esteem, so that the compromise with discomfort turns out to be a compromise with truth.

18

Una phoned after breakfast. "Paul. I'm at the nursery school. I've just dropped Betsy off. I'm speaking in the teacher's office. I do as much phoning as I can away from home just to give those bastards the pip. They even listen in on my conversations with the fishmonger. Listen, darling, you leave tomorrow and we've hardly seen you."

"I'm so sorry, Una. I've just been hanging around the house most of the time so that whenever my father feels up to it I can be with him."

"Of course. I understand, darling. But he goes to sleep quite early, doesn't he? So why don't we pick you up around nine tonight. Etienne van Dongen will be here, he's up from the Cape to see his publisher, and I know you'll enjoy talking to him."

"I can drive over myself."

"Nonsense, darling. We'll pick you up at nine. 'Bye." She was gone.

After lunch Eugene came to visit his father. They sat

out on the terrace with a jug of Rosie's lemon squash, but it was difficult to push the conversation along. Eugene told him that there was not much change in his father's condition, he was slowly failing, it was just a matter of time. Because of the unnatural circumstances, he was finding his usual fund of comfort to next-of-kin inept, and an uncomfortable silence fell between them. Eugene drained down his lemon drink, shook hands, made as if to say something, thought better of it, and left.

His father drowsed most of the afternoon. Sister sat in an armchair in the sitting room crocheting baby clothes for her daughter, who, she explained, was expecting. In the kitchen Rosie was busy making shortbread for him to take back to the children.

He felt as he had as a boy, when everyone in the house was occupied and he at a loose end, wandering from room to room vaguely hoping to find something to engage him.

From the study window he could see his watcher in the black Morris. He seemed to be a bull-like young man with a thick neck, pink face, and pale hair. Watching his watcher, he felt a sudden spurt of rage rise in him. I hope it's hot and stuffy in that little car and the bastard is sweltering.

The afternoon limped blankly along. He went out into the garden and tried to read, but only his eyes passed over the words, his mind moving about in the flat sunshine as if looking for shade. He rose and went indoors to the cool of the study. Margot looked down at him with mild irony. She and the boys seemed far away in time as well as space, belonging in another existence unconnected with the present he now occupied. He dragged his attention away from the restless thrust of his unease, and concentrated on an article in the *British Medical Journal*, knowing that only the rigorous demands of rational scientific material were capable of engaging him, all other forms of distraction, music, novels, serving only as avenues leading directly back to the source of his anguish.

For a merciful hour he forgot where he was, his concentration wholly engaged by problems of "Pulmonary Complications Following Mitral Valvotomy." Rosie's knock

104

at the door reminded him it was tea time. She came in, bearing no tea tray, looking perturbed.

"Master Paul, there's a boy from the greengrocer in the yard. I told him we didn't order any fruit or vegetables, but he says he wants to see the master. I told him the old master is sick in bed, so he says he'll see the young master." She shook her head, exasperated. "I said to him—if you bring an order to the wrong house, why should I disturb my master—but he won't go. He's not cheeky or anything like that, but he says he's not going until the master comes out."

Listening to her, he felt a dull boom resound in a cavern of his awareness, recognizing it almost—an echo from some event that had occurred at another time, like thunder rumbling in the pause that follows after lightning has struck. Uneasy, he rose and followed Rosie to the kitchen.

Outside the back door a black man sat on a delivery bicycle, one foot resting on the step. His basket was filled with bananas, pawpaws, oranges, eggplants, onions, green peppers, all vivid in the sun-filled afternoon. The name of the local greengrocer was painted in large letters round the metal rack which held the basket in place. The delivery man was dressed in washed-out gray flannels, a shabby checked shirt, and brand-new American basketball sneakers. On his head was a peaked khaki cap.

The delivery man said, "Good afternoon, Master."

He responded to the greeting, suspended momentarily in a brief hiatus of hope at the sheer ordinariness of the scene. The man removed his cap, and in a heart-shifting split second, he recognized Benedict Mashaba.

Rosie still lurked, filled with misgiving, at his shoulder. He said, "Don't worry, Rosie, I'll straighten it out," and she went back to her baking.

He said, "Benedict."

"Doctor, I am sorry to disturb you in this way." He smiled ironically at the trappings of his assumed role. "But it is a matter of great urgency, Doctor, or I would not interfere with you at a time like this."

Waiting in the kitchen doorway, he felt almost as if he had been expecting this visit, as if the menace of it had

105

accompanied him since the moment he had stepped onto the airplane.

Gesturing toward the kitchen with his head, Benedict asked, "The cook, is she reliable? How long has she worked here?"

He sighed as his internal darkness rose up like some slow-breaking wave. He said, "Since I was born."

Benedict said, businesslike, "That's OK then." Leaning forward he spoke in a low voice. "Doctor, we don't like to ask you this, but there is no other way for us." He patted his shirt pocket. "I have a letter here that must get to London. It is a matter of great urgency. We have been using a certain address in London, but we don't think it is safe anymore because several things we have sent there recently have not arrived. The party at this address, in Islington, must be warned of this. They must be told that a new mailing address must be set up. And they must get this document—it is very important." He patted his breast pocket again.

Listening to Benedict, he felt, not fear, but an engulfing sadness as though he mourned for himself. He stood in the bright afternoon sun with the basket of fruit and vegetables imprinted in bright pigment on his retina. He thought, I am trapped; if I help him I shall despair and if I refuse him I shall despair.

Benedict waited for a response, and receiving none, continued with urgency. "Doctor—forgive us for putting this extra load on you. We know what you have already gone through, we know what you are going through. But Doctor, terrible things are happening to our people, and we must look for help wherever we can find it." He reached inside his shirt and extracted a flimsy folded sheet of lined paper torn from a cheap writing pad. "This letter had been smuggled out of the Pretoria jail. It is from the wife of Ezekiel Mphahlele—he is imprisoned on Robben Island for life. He was convicted for allegedly going to a foreign country to receive military training. Now they have arrested her, and she has a very bad heart and they are torturing her, Doctor, torturing her. She is going to die if they are not made to stop." He waited for the weight of his information to sink in, then went on. "One of the African guards in the jail has become so disgusted by what he has witnessed that he offered to help her, and he smuggled out this letter. Now you know, Doctor, that not a single newspaper in South Africa is allowed to print any information about detainees—the law forbids it—they are liable to prosecution if they do. But if you can get this letter to London for us, our contacts there will see that it gets into the British press and is widely publicized—Mphahlele is well known overseas and there will be protests from prominent people—and then our government will have to account for this woman." He spoke with the letter held out in his hand, proffering it. "This is our only hope. Otherwise, she is going to die." He paused, then added, "She has five small children."

In the ensuing silence he noticed, dully, how pleasing the line and color of a taut purple eggplant was against the ridges of the deep yellow of a pawpaw. He looked up at Benedict. "How do you know I am safe? They have been keeping a watch on me since I got here."

"I have discussed this with my group. It did not seem likely to us that the Special Branch would be suspicious of you. They know your hands are really tied because you left on an exit permit—they would not expect you take any risk, with your family six thousand miles away and your father dying. And you've got a British passport now, haven't you, Doctor?"

He nodded.

Benedict said, "Well, that will protect you too."

He said, "They've arrested people with British passports before."

Benedict was silent, tapping on the edge of the basket with the letter.

He said, "What if I memorize the contents of the letter and tell them about it when I get to London."

Benedict shook his head. "No good. It wouldn't have the same—authority—as the original letter. The Special Branch could easily deny it."

In the kitchen beyond them, Rosie could be heard clattering baking pans at the sink.

107

Benedict said, "Look here, Doctor. We know we are asking a lot of you. And we know that your heart is full of sorrow because your father is old and dying and you are far from your wife and your children. So look here. I will leave this letter with you, and it is up to you to decide whether you will take it or not. If you take it, it must go to this address." He showed him a scrap of paper with an address in Islington printed on it in childish capitals. "You should memorize the address. It should be delivered by hand, and they must be advised to establish a new mailing address for the future and to advise us of it through the usual channels." As he spoke, the shabby delivery man took on the authority of a militant organizer, his clothes and basket of fruit and vegetables appearing as mere stage props. He looked stern, proffering both pieces of paper, waiting for them to be taken.

He stood, listening to Benedict, immobile in the doorway, without will, as though he were a puppet waiting for strings to be pulled to jerk him into action.

Still holding out the scraps of paper, Benedict went on, "If, on the other hand, Doctor, you feel it would be preferable not to take the letter with you, we will understand." He shrugged, placing the whole weight of the history of the white man's infamy squarely on the shoulders of the white man who stood, unresponsive, in the doorway of the splendidly equipped kitchen where an old black woman worked as she had been doing for nearly half a century. "In that case, you must burn the letter. It is of no use to anyone in this country. It can only serve its purpose if it can get to England. Otherwise it is useless. Burn it then."

The scraps of paper were thrust into his hand, the strings were tugged by the puppet master and his fingers closed around them. Benedict said, "Read the letter—it will help you make up your mind. You don't need to tell me your decision, Doctor. We will know, whichever way it works out. And it is better not to discuss it with anyone else, even Barney Bateman. The fewer people that know, the safer we all are."

He put his cap back on. A chill had crept up between them; there was none of the camaraderie of their previous encounter when they had both felt they were on the same
108

side of the fence. They were both aware now that one of them was inside, invulnerable if he chose, while the other was, always had been, on the outside with little or no choice at all. Benedict said, as if dismissing him, "Better ask the old woman to take all this fruit and stuff out of the basket. And then maybe she should walk with me as far as the front gate as if she is my auntie."

He turned and called into the kitchen, "Rosie, can you help us with this—bring us a basket please."

She came, bringing a wide flat basket from the pantry, and the fruit and vegetables were transferred from the bicycle. She worked in silence. Benedict said something to her in the vernacular. She nodded, accepting her role in their small charade with an unquestioning quietness that moved him. She said to Benedict, "Wait a moment while I put all this stuff away in the pantry."

Benedict said, "Good-bye then, Doctor. And whatever happens, good luck." He did not shake hands, merely touched the peak of his cap.

Rosie came out and the two of them walked away together down the driveway, he pushing the bicycle, the two of them engaging in a loud animated conversation with much gesturing. He watched them disappear round the curve of the driveway.

Back in the study, he sat down at the desk, the two scraps of paper still grasped in his hand. He looked down at the meaningless words printed on the good heavy paper of the *British Medical Journal*. He looked up at the portrait of Margot on the wall. Now he found that because of the two flimsy bits of paper he was holding, the whole emphasis of his being had shifted, altered. Now, Margot was his reality. The palms of his hands recalled their familiarity with the dark gloss of her hair, the curve of her high cheekbones beneath the fine-grained pale skin of her face; he smelled the fresh-washed soapy smell of her, heard the low calm tone of her voice. Her presence was so immediately and directly discernible to him, that almost he expected the children to join them. *They* were the substance of his actuality, while father dying down the hall, Sister with her coy crisp little ways, Rosie and Benedict—complete strangers chatting away together like blood kin—the grubby paper scraps in his hand, the sunlight lying indiscriminate over it all, now assumed the insubstantiality of a nightmare.

Rosie, coming in with the tea tray, found him still sitting there, elbows on the desk, eyes and forehead enclosed in the vise of his clasped hands. She placed the tray on the desk and asked tentatively, "Paulie, is it something very bad?"

He looked up at his old nurse who was caught with him in his nightmare, feeling the poverty of his access to solace and reassurance as a dry pit filled with old bones lying between them. He said, automatically, "It will be all right, Rosie, don't worry, it will be all right."

Uneasy, she watched him pour his tea before she left the room.

He drank his tea, staring at the portrait of Margot as though by the sheer force of his longing he could will himself back with her in the soft enveloping English rain and away from the consuming heat and threat of Africa. He found that his mind was repeating with a rhythmic chant the address he had glimpsed on the bit of paper.

Top Flat
22 Cheltenham Gardens
Islington
London. N. I.

He thought, without my knowledge or consent it has lodged itself in my memory. I shall probably never forget it now, even if I want to. He looked at last at the two documents. The address was written in the painstaking hand of someone with a few laborious years of elementary schooling.

Top Flat
22 Cheltenham Gardens
Islington
London, N. I.

He ripped it across and across again, dropped the fragments into an ashtray, struck a match and set them alight, watching them curl up, char, and blacken. He touched an ashen shred and watched it disintegrate into sooty specks while his mind continued its unwelcome pounding chant:

Top Flat
Twenty-two
Cheltenham Gardens
London.

Now he unfolded the sheet of lined paper and read its message penciled in sloping cursive letters.

To Whom It May Concern
Please note that during my questioning I am being subjected to cruel and inhuman treatment. I have been made to stand erect for periods up to 24 hrs with my hands held up above my head. If I bring my hands down or fall asleep I am beaten and kicked and sworn at. I am kept during all this questioning time without even a drop of water. Even though they know I have a bad heart they have taken my medicine away from me and do not allow me to see the doctor. If I am not helped soon I am sure I will die and I worry all the time about my five children aged from 11 yrs to 2 yrs. Signed, Feb. 11th.

Mary Mphahlele.

As he refolded the note along the creases that grubbily crisscrossed it, he noticed the shaking of his hands and the sickening thudding of his heart. He sat for so long looking at the ashtray littered with the charred fragments, at the box of matches, at the portrait of Margot, that when Rosie knocked at the door to announce dinner he found he was sitting in darkness. He turned on a lamp, stood up, looked hopelessly around the room, then removed from the bookshelf a thick blue-bound volume—*The Principles and Practice of Medicine* by Sir Stanley Davidson. Opening it at page twenty-two he slipped the letter in, closed it, and replaced it on the shelf. In the dim light of the lamp Margot's portrait hovered. He stood

111

in front of it and stared at it until it began to disintegrate into the individual brushstrokes his mother had laid down upon the canvas so many years ago, an agglomeration of particles, grains, chips of pigments, fragments formless and meaningless. Rosie knocked again, and he followed her to the dining room wondering how he would be able to eat the food she had prepared for him with such love and skill.

After dinner he sat for a while in the sickroom. Though the inside of his chest felt bruised, he tried to amuse the old man with anecdotes about the boys and succeeded in making him smile once or twice. He could see that his father was also making an effort: he was breathless, his lips were blue, and he asked for Sister to be called in to give him his digitalis. They gave him a sedative as well and made him comfortable for the night. Then he went back to the study and stared at the spine of *The Principles and Practice of Medicine* by Sir Stanley Davidson, while in his brain a ball seemed to bounce out an idiot beat: *TOP flat, TWENty-two CHELTenham Gardens, LONdon.*

When Barney came to fetch him he went with him feeling a weight drag in his chest.

When they turned out of their street he said, "Look in the rearview mirror, Barney. Is there a black Morris Minor behind us?"

"Yes, old chap, there is."

"Shouldn't we try and give them the slip?"

"Oh. So the bastards did put a watch on you. I thought they might. Don't worry old man, it's all right to come to my place. They know I'm your lawyer and I handle your affairs. I hope you've been careful though."

"I've only been out twice." He told Barney of his visit to someone in Fordsburg, wondering if Barney also knew about Zainab, but needing it to be bracketed in privacy. Barney laughed enormously when he heard how he had outwitted his guard, slapping his great thighs with relish. "Good—so the stupid bastard snoozed all afternoon in the stifling car and you weren't even home. I like that, I really like that, although even asphyxiation is too good for the swine."

"But, Barney, I'm a little worried about the other time." He described his shopping expedition, his encounter with B⌐nedict Mashaba. "My first reaction was fear. I wanted to run. I thought, they've planted him and they'll try to incriminate me. Then I was disgusted with myself. Benedict's a decent chap—I've known him for years. I understood then how effective their techniques are—how easily one can be contaminated with fear and suspicion."

"But all the same, you didn't say anything to him I hope."

His viscera slipped uneasily. He ached to tell Barney about the afternoon's business. "Why not, do you know something about him?"

Barney said, "No no, old chap. I'm pretty sure he's straight. He's devoted to Abel, and worries all the time about the fact that he's in for life."

"He told me he helps support Abel's wife and kids."

"I'm sure he does."

He said, "I gave him some money to give to them."

They stopped at a traffic light. Barney was silent. He patted all his jacket pockets and said, "Damn and blast, I must have left my bloody cigars at the office." The light turned green. He changed gear and they drove on.

"Shouldn't I have done that, Barney?"

Barney sighed. He said, "Oh Christ, Paul. Look what they have done to us, how we are corrupted. Our slightest gestures of humanity are fear-ridden. We're simply afraid to act in a plain ethical spirit anymore because it makes us vulnerable. We're all turning into self-protective organisms concerned only with our own survival. This is their greatest triumph, Paul. This is where their power lies. I've known Benedict for twenty years, and here am I afraid to vouch for his reliability. You see, just having his brother in jail gives them a hold over him, so who knows? I have no reason to doubt him, yet I cannot trust him. We're all suspect. Christ, I don't know why I stay on here. They've won. Hands down."

For the next half mile they drove in silence. Then Barney asked, "How much did you give him?"

"All I had in my pocket. About nineteen rand I think it was."

"Well, let's assume it was OK. Christ, man, it's too horrible, you get so suspicious you can't live with yourself. And what they've done to the Africans is even worse. It's no use saying so-and-so's a decent fellow, he'd never turn informer. They're poor. They can buy them off, offer them more money than they could ever dream of earning. Or they threaten them, we'll see you lose your job, kaffir, or, we'll let your sister out of jail if you work with us, kaffir. The most vulnerable ones are those who've been politically involved. They torture them and then offer them freedom if they'll agree to work for the Special Branch. None of them can trust each other anymore. I don't know how it's ever going to be possible for them to organize any resistance. How is a black freedom movement going to arise with all the politically aware Africans in prison or in exile, and the masses terrorized and riddled with informers?"

"Benedict said to me that when his black brothers in the new African states are strong enough they will come down to liberate this country."

Barney asked, "How long is that going to take? How much spiritual erosion will there be until then? All those African republics have such terrible problems of their own, how the hell are they going to be able to liberate South Africa?"

"Perhaps they'll find they have to do it before they put their own houses in order. It's politically and morally important for the rest of Africa—South Africa is a thorn in their flesh. They have no choice anymore—they have to drive apartheid out of the continent."

"Oh Christ, Paul," Barney spoke with a weight of weariness, "I get depressed just thinking about it. We all know damn well that there's increasing guerrilla action on the borders every day—even though they do all they can to keep that kind of news out of the papers. Those guerrillas are dedicated and desperate—I've heard some hair-raising stories of what they've done to border patrols. It's a real problem to the government—they're starting to replace police patrols with highly trained soldiers. And now with Portugal relinquishing her African colonies, we and Rhodesia are going to be vulnerable on the Portuguese borders too." He sighed. "But what will it all amount to, anyway, when the crux of it all is the millions of British and American capital invested in South Africa? *That's* the real power. All that gabble and votes of censure at the United Nations—all those countries piously condemning apartheid while they're engaged in selling armaments to our government under the counter to ensure that white rule is sustained! What really counts is the gold and the diamonds and the copper and the uranium and all the other natural resources with which this glorious republic is blessed and cursed. I have a need to believe there will be justice and freedom here someday—but God knows how it's going to come about."

He remained silent, not wanting to speak his thought out loud to his friend—the mood in a minor enough key without the addition of a further somber chord—not wishing to say to Barney, "However it comes about, it's a black struggle now, and the whites in Africa are doomed, no matter where their hearts lie."

Barney turned into the driveway of his house and parked the car.

The *stoep* ran the length of the house. One end of it was covered with a pergola over which a luxuriant grapevine had been trained. Half-ripe bunches of grapes glowed pale among the black leaves. The bright moon filtered through the vine, splashing onto a table with wicker chairs grouped around it. Here Una sat talking to a short, fair, bearded man with eyes that could be seen to be remarkably blue even by moonlight. On the table were balloon glasses, a bottle of cognac, a bowl heaped with figs, tangerines, grapes, a board with an assortment of cheeses.

Una embraced him. Warm, soft, her cheek smooth,

soap-scented, her breath rich with the bouquet of cognac. What comfort to lie down with one's head on those abundant breasts, to close one's eyes and rest there.

She said, "I think you must have met Etienne here about a hundred years ago, darling."

He shook hands with the bearded man, said, "I know I will carry about with me forever those poems of yours that I was made to learn by heart at school."

They all laughed. Etienne said, "I'm still at it, Doctor, still scribbling away at my poetry as if my life depended on it, which perhaps it does, though fewer and fewer folk read it." He spoke perfect, formal English with a heavy Cape Afrikaans accent.

Una said, "Come now, Etienne, we all know that poets have to write poetry whether anyone reads it or not."

Etienne chewed a grape with deliberation, removed the seeds and placed them meticulously on his plate. "Yes, my dear Una, that is my destiny and my tragedy."

Barney said, "Your tragedy? Man, I wish I were a poet instead of a lawyer. A poet just has to sit there watching the antics of the world, commenting on human folly, while I am embroiled at the center of all the folly."

"True, Barney, but my tragedy, alas, is my mother tongue. I think in Afrikaans, I feel in Afrikaans, my very soul is Afrikaans. But my sentiments are such that the vast majority of those who understand Afrikaans eschew my poetry. My people, 'die Volk,' do not read my poetry. Worse, they despise my poetry. I am scourged and vilified for it." He spoke with the extreme circumspection of one who is rather drunk. The brandy glass cradled in his palm, he swirled the amber liquid round and round, observing the small maelstrom he caused.

"Look at all of us sitting around this table, drinking excellent aged cognac, the moonlight sifting down on us through the vine; purple figs, black grapes, orange tangerines in this bowl. Civilized human beings. Is there not something noble about our aspect? This cognac, man's ingenuity combined with nature's prodigality. Our thoughts and conversation lofty. Who would think, looking at us, eh, that we
116

are debris thrown up by a tragic time in a tragic place. That we are all trapped in a cloaca of history."

There was laughter. Barney filled glasses. Una's plump managing hands, doused in moonlight, pared the fibrous skin off a tangerine, deftly divided it and offered the segments around. Etienne sliced a wedge of cheese and bit contemplatively into it.

He observed the vivid scene, feeling the heat of the brandy suffusing his blood. As he drank, the clarity of the blue textbook of medicine began mercifully to blur.

Una's mellifluous voice; "... just look at us ... a motley assortment. Etienne's ancestors arriving here from Holland eight generations ago, Barney's and mine from Eastern Europe three generations ago, Paul's from England four generations ago."

"Perhaps we ought not to forget, even though they are not drinking cognac on the *stoep* with us," Barney said, "our African brothers who have been here since the dawn of history."

Etienne said, "I am prepared to admit that, even though my family came here in the seventeenth century with the earliest Dutch settlers, next to the blacks I am a relative newcomer. But I challenge anyone to deny that my roots are as deep in the soil of Africa as a black man's." He filled his glass. He looked round at all of them, smiled, said, "I think I am becoming somewhat intoxicated; I am a drunken Afrikaans poet, but this does not detract from the truth of my words."

As his eyes grew accustomed to the half light he could see that the fairness of the poet's hair was more white than yellow. Etienne continued. "Let me tell you all about an incident that occurred in New York which moved me very deeply. I spent some years in the States on a fellowship from one of those fabulous moneyed foundations that are the modern equivalent of the old aristocratic patrons of the arts. I was translating a volume of my poems into English. Ah," he shook his head mournfully, "a sorry labor. A translation of a poem is like a snapshot of a Van Gogh. The form is there, but the texture, the unspoken, the implied, the nuances, the

117

subtlety—all lost. However, I must not digress. At a cocktail party in Manhattan I was introduced to a black man; a compatriot of mine, my hostess told me. An exile, a revolutionary of some sort, he seemed to flit about between England and Africa and America raising money. To what purpose? I shuddered to inquire. We got talking. We had both been away from home for a long time. And I tell you, our nostalgia, our *mal du pays* was identical. We sat there, this Bantu and I, on a soft white leather couch, by a window overlooking this man-made miracle which is New York, the skyscrapers and bridges picked out in lights against the night sky. And we talked of what our hearts ached for. We talked of the spectacular desolation of the Karroo; we talked of the highveld in spring, the light dry pristine air that is more intoxicating than the finest cognac. The crooked thorn trees, the native huts, the little crystal rivers running over their stony beds. We talked of Capetown, the green mountains sloping down to the blue of Table Bay, the forests of Knysna, the Wilderness, Plettenberg Bay. I tell you, this Bantu and I, that night we were brothers. There was no talk of Nationalists or apartheid or gold or foreign investments. We talked of fundamentals, our roots. We were both drawn to our country as the blood is drawn to the heart." He took a pull at his brandy, rolled it around his mouth and swallowed, breathing heavily.

They were all silent on the *stoep*.

"I never knew this before, about having roots," he said, his voice sounding gruff, unfamiliar in his ears, "until I stepped off the plane after ten years, and knew—knew that I was back. In Africa."

Barney said, "What do you mean, old man?"

Etienne said, "I'll tell you what he means, Barney. He knew. He knew in the biblical sense of the word. He knew, not with his brain, but with his gut and his blood and his heart, with something deep and primitive in him, he knew."

He felt gratitude to the poet. He said, "That must be how it was. It was such a strong feeling it almost knocked me over. And yet, at the same time, I also know that I hate this

118

country. It's an evil place—more evil, I think, for being so beautiful."

Etienne hunched himself up in his chair, seemed to grow smaller, to draw within himself. He said, "It is not the country you hate, Doctor, it is what has been perpetrated upon it. They do not rule, this government. To rule is to have the support of the population. They do not rule. They merely impose their will. They violate this land and its people, blacks and whites. But we are talking of something transient. What I love, what I carry about with me in the nerves and marrow and bloodstream, is the Africa that was here before them; that will be here long after they have passed."

He leaned forward, an aging, bearded gnome. "*They* do not consider me a true Afrikaner because I do not support their ideology. Barney here does not consider me a true South African because I will not join the fight against *them*. As a poet I am concerned with searching for the truth. The Nationalists are evil of course, but they are rich and powerful, and finally, they are stupid. They will not be defeated by revolutionaries inside or outside the country. They will be defeated by their own stupidity. The country is booming, and there is a serious shortage of white skilled labor. So they will be forced to start employing blacks to do the skilled work, and they will have to pay them skilled wages. And the blacks will then develop a sense of their own identity, and they will struggle to organize trade unions and so on and so forth—we are all familiar with the pattern of the rise of the industrial working class.

"But let me tell you something that perhaps you romantics do not realize, that perhaps you will not like to hear. This is the time in history of the culture of the masses. You should see the United States, the peak, the very acme of mass culture, where everything is reduced to the lowest common denominator to make it accessible to the largest number of individuals. And it will be this way soon in Europe too. The masses are mindless; they take for granted the incredible genius of man that has gone into the making of

119

civilization, and it has no value for them. They use it and they throw it away like an empty box. Their aspirations, manipulated by the powers that be, are all material and self-gratifying. There is no spiritual evolution to balance the technological evolution. There is no sense of awe or wonder either for civilization or for nature. So here is my thesis. When the blacks of our country have thrown off the yoke of oppression, what they will all aspire to will be the gross materialism of mass culture. Television, refrigerators, motor cars poisoning the pure air, factory-schools and universities turning mass men off the assembly line of education."

Barney said, "But Etienne—as awful as you make it sound, surely it is preferable to abject poverty and absolute oppression."

Etienne sagged in his chair, surveyed them all with a stare of intense blue. "One would have hoped that the so-called third world could have learned a lesson from the other two, before it was too late, before they committed the same folly. However," he shrugged, "who am I to judge human folly, a mere drunken Afrikaans poet, writing in a bastardized language no one understands, no one reads. Watching my own country raped by disciples of the devil, and knowing that the crusaders who will bring salvation come to transform the black people into consumers of the goods of technology. They will come bearing TVs and tape recorders and tin-openers and detergents and not, alas, the Holy Grail."

Etienne leaned unsteadily forward to cut a piece of cheese, missed his aim, the knife hitting the cheeseboard with a loud clatter. Una took it from him, sliced off a wedge of cheese, pared it, and handed it to him. He ate it, gulped some brandy, sat up straight in his chair, said, "Forgive me, Doctor. I should not be talking this way. I have been told that your father is dying and that they have graciously allowed you back in your mother country for just one week. Forgive me. Before I go, and I must leave now, let me assure you that in spite of what I say, I am still compelled to go on writing my poetry, which of course somehow denies the pessimism of what I have been saying. Just as Barney's and Una's good fight for the dignity of our Bantu brothers denies

120

it. Just as your own devotion to your duty and your assumption of the heavy burden of your unjust punishment denies it. Just as this white moonlight denies the dark."

He stood up, swayed, steadied himself at the table. "Ach–if only you rednecks understood Afrikaans properly, I could tell you what I mean by quoting some of my poems. As it is," he held up his glass, "I propose a toast to the affirmation of the spirit of man, in spite of his baseness and his tragic limitations." He clinked glasses with all of them. "And let us drink too, to our belief that the purpose of the universe is–that man should behave as if there is a purpose to the universe."

They drank. Etienne shook hands formally with everyone. Barney, supporting him, led him to the car, packed him in, and drove off.

The moon moved across the sky, behind the trees at the back of the house, leaving them in clotted darkness. He and Una sat in silence. A small sigh found its way out of Una's amplitude into the night air. She said, "I don't think Barney understands what Etienne means. But I do. Do you, Paul?"

He shook his head, gloomy.

"I thought he would entertain you, but he's depressed you. I'm sorry, darling."

He said, "I'm not depressed, Una, I'm lost."

"Lost, darling?"

"So much has happened to me since I stepped onto the plane in London last week."

"I know–it's been a hard time for you."

"No. That's not what I mean. I don't mean the particulars I've experienced all week: it's as though I've been forced to pull together the meaning of events I've been concerned with all my life." The cognac seemed to light up his confusion with slippery glimpses of lucidity. "Now I have to try to understand what I've done, in order to understand what I must do."

Una took his hand in hers. He studied her hand, large, well-shaped, with short clipped nails, cushioned, covered with fine white skin.

121

He said, "I think I understand what Etienne means, but only outwardly, and I have to try to understand inwardly as well, if it's to make any sense."

"Sense, darling?"

"Yes. What's the use of saying—I understand—I believe—I have new insights—without then behaving in a way that is directed by these new insights—measures up to them?"

"But you've always acted on what you believed."

He held her hand up to his cheek. "No. Not really. I've never stopped to consider my beliefs. I have a great dark area of my consciousness that I've dragged around with me and never stopped to examine. Now I have no alternative. I can't let events dominate me anymore—I have to try and retrieve something from—from all my circumstances."

"Will this help you solve your problems?"

He smiled in the dark. "Not solve them, but deal with them perhaps."

"I'm not sure I understand what you mean. I'm very literal, Paul. What will you do? Be psychoanalyzed, or take up Buddhism or philosophy or something like that? I believe Ismael Pillay is studying philosophy in prison."

He said, "Philosophy. Buddhism. Analysis. Man is the object of all of them. I don't know how I'll do it, I've told you, Una, I'm lost." He took her hand and placed it palm downward in his own, marveling at its remarkableness. "I only know that I can't drag around with it anymore."

She said, "Well, darling, I suppose once one realizes one is lost, one starts trying to find the way out."

He said, "Through the dark."

She said, "I suppose it's the only way."

He sat, her hand warm in his palm. The garden was black now, the grapevine no longer casting shadows.

Later, he said, "Una—do you think Gilbert is in love with Margot?"

She removed her hand. "In love with her?" She was silent for a while. "I don't know, Paul. I do know that he's always adored her."

He had drunk too much cognac. He felt soft, floundering, in the warm dark night. He said, "D'you know, if they were in bed together, at this moment, I wouldn't mind. Just as long as she's at the airport to meet me on Sunday morning."

"She'll be there, darling."

The headlights of the car swept the driveway. The car door slammed. Barney came back onto the *stoep*. "I left Etienne with his sister tucking him into bed." He stood, leaning against a pillar. "I can't say I understood what the hell that was all about, specially that bit about devils and Holy Grails. But still, he's a fine chap, Etienne, an Afrikaner in a million."

Una said, "It's no wonder he needs to drink. It's a much greater struggle for an Afrikaner to reach the sort of understanding he has, than for people with our kind of liberal-radical conditioning. It comes easily to us, but he's had to battle his way out of the Boer tradition, the Calvinism, the prejudice, the meanness of vision."

Barney said, "There are so few of them. They have to be heroes. They have to start off by opposing their families, their whole tradition. Look at Piet Visser, a son of one of the oldest, most distinguished Afrikaans families, in jail for life. A great lawyer and a great human being who has chosen to end out his days in jail. Because when they say—for life—that is just what they mean. There's no hope of remission of his sentence. He's in his sixties, and they'll never let him out. They wouldn't even let him out for a couple of hours to go to his son's funeral."

"We've talked a lot about Piet Visser in London," he said. "All those months he was hiding from the police, he had the chance to escape from the country, but he wouldn't go. He made his choice, fully aware of what the consequences would be. In London, some people are saying he chose to make a martyr of himself. Others, that his example is an inspiration to the Africans, a symbol of hope, an instance that not everyone is running out on them. Some of them say it was his duty to have escaped because he is politically ineffective in jail, and if he were out of the country he could still be working against apartheid."

"Which of those is your opinion, darling?"

123

"Well, at the time, my feeling was that by remaining in South Africa and risking capture he was playing the game according to their rules, allowing them to decide the moves and the penalties. And it seemed to me that once one has decided that their rules are immoral, then their penalties are not valid and one should not submit to them. But now," he raised his hands in a gesture of helplessness, dropped them in his lap, "now, I am not sure about anything anymore. Perhaps—each one has to work his destiny out in his own way. And by leaving the country, Piet might have felt he was denying the purpose of his life; so for him this was the only way to act—he had no choice."

"All this is too vague and abstruse for me, old chap. I reckon I am a simple pragmatic lawyer, and for a saint like Piet to be in jail for life, is wrong, wrong, wrong."

Una said, "Of course, darling, but Paul means for Piet himself, perhaps it was the right choice to make."

"You two give rightness too many subtle qualities for me. I don't think I could function in the courts if I were aware of all the finer shades." Leaning against the pillar, a large burly man with fading red hair, his fists clenching, unclenching, he sounded weary, unhopeful. He said, "Paul, by the way, I noticed your friend is parked at the corner in his little black Morris."

He said, "Well, it's late, and I'm rather drunk, so let's take the poor swine home."

He was enfolded in Una's warmth and softness for a moment, Una, mother of mothers.

"We'll pick you up at ten tomorrow to take you to the airport, darling." She looked at him sternly, as she looked at her children when she was forced to divulge to them some grim truth.

Barney drove him home. The little black car tailed them like a buzzing fly.

19

He let himself in through the front door. The house was quiet, everyone asleep.

Within him, something raced, sending out small signals of distress that whirred against the walls of his chest and abdomen. He went upstairs, undressed, brushed his teeth, came down again, took a bottle of cognac out of the sideboard, poured himself a drink. He sat in the dark sitting room, sipping, waiting for the potency of the liquor to subdue the circles of urgency that spun and spun in him. The curtains were drawn across the french windows, the garden and sky blotted out. He poured another drink.

I'll be hungover tomorrow. Barney and Una will have to drag me to the car, push me onto the plane. He felt heavy, hopeless. After another drink the tension loosed into a dense weight.

He went up to his room, lay still in the bed. The same room, the same bed, the same darkness in which he had slept the nights of his childhood and youth lightly away.

Not the same darkness at all. It had another quality, palpable, oppressive. Try to sleep, have to be up early in the morning to catch the plane. Back to Margot and the boys.

Margot and the boys had no reality now in the impenetrable blackness. Drowsing from the brandy, his eyes closed, he lurched suddenly awake remembering a printed form they had given him at the airport when he had come through Immigration. The official had said it must be completed and handed back before he left the country. In the dark he could hear his heart knocking against his rib cage. He turned on the lamp, got out of bed, searched through his papers, located the form among the pages of his passport. The information required was to do with currency regulations. Relieved, he filled it in, got back into bed, and turned off the light.

Now he was wide awake. He listened to his heartbeat, his breathing, his eyelashes brushing against the pillow sounding like batwings close by. Benedict Mashaba's face loomed up in front of him. Now it seemed absurd to believe it was mere chance that they had met the other day in town. The whole encounter was patently a setup, and this afternoon's little drama was a further entrapment. Obviously Benedict was a police informer; perhaps his job was to try to find out if he was in contact with any of the exile underground groups in London. Whatever their scheme was, he had been a naive fool to fall for it the first time and give him that money. Barney thought so too but didn't want to alarm him. He had walked straight into their trap.

The blue spine of Sir Stanley Davidson's *The Principles and Practice of Medicine* jolted him as he debated. That letter—it was obviously genuine. Benedict was no informer. Abel Mashaba's brother would never be an informer. Yet it was Barney who had said that the families of political prisoners were most vulnerable to the blackmail of the Special Branch. He sat up in bed, sweating, and turned on the light. In the pleasant bedroom in which he had lightly slept his youth away he felt as boxed in, enclosed, as powerless as he had been in his prison cell. He saw it was only three

126

o'clock; four hours to get through until Rosie would come in with the morning tea.

He rose, put on his dressing gown and went to the study. He took Sir Stanley Davidson from the bookshelf, opened it at page twenty-two half hoping that the letter would not be there and he had imagined the whole episode. It was there; crisscrossed by its grubby creases. He took it back to the bedroom and sat down on the bed. He could not unfold it: it was as if the muffled screams and stench of the jail would well up out of it and inundate the room. With the letter in his hand, solitarily awake in the predawn darkness, he was besieged by the possibilities that confronted him whatever choice he made.

He remembered the simplicity of holding the match to the other document and seeing it obliterated in a few licks of flame. It was so easy. They could not expect him to take any more risks. Conflicting voices assailed him. He heard Benedict saying—*we must look for help wherever we can find it*. He saw the aging poet swaying in the moonlight under the grapevine, the cognac slopping about in his glass as he declaimed—*the purpose of the universe is that man should behave as if there is a purpose to the universe*. From the dark of ten years ago he heard the colonel's voice insinuating—*don't you realize that you are being used by these people? how can it be worth it to you to suffer like this for people who consider you expendable?* He thought, as he had thought in the car with Barney, it is their struggle—the black man's struggle—why should I involve myself in it now?

His head ached; the little inane chant hammered at his temples—*top* flat, *twenty*-two, *chelt*enham gardens, *lon*don. He stood up and paced the bedroom as he had paced his prison cell. When the walls seemed to be pressing in closer and closer, he stopped at last by the bureau and took from a drawer the presents he had bought for his children; the mask, the shield and assegai, the box with the ostrich egg nestling in tissue. As his mind ranged about for all the reasons which would justify burning the letter, his hands explored the skin of the shield, his fingers nervously prodding, investigating interstices where the cowhide was plaited and woven. He put the shield down and took up the ostrich egg; looking at it he felt his small son's arms about his neck, the warm round cheek soft against his own, the voice husky in his ear reminding him again and again not to forget to come home with an ostrich egg. Carefully, he replaced it in the box, looked, helpless, at the letter in his hand, slipped it into the pocket of his pajama jacket, got back into bed and turned off the light. He lay back, willing the obliteration of sleep. But instead of sleep only his inner darkness rose up to join the black night. He was entombed in it; it pressed down on him making breathing difficult. Father dying in his room along the hall—he thought, dying must be easier than this.

What can they do to me? I have British citizenship. That's no real protection; they've imprisoned others with British citizenship. In his brandy-logged despair he saw the Immigration Department's exit turnstile as a distant unattainable gateway that would need a Blake to depict the hallowed quality it now had for him. He saw Laurel and Hardy appearing in the radiant pearly gateway, one on each side, one taking each arm and leading him away. His mouth was dry as he listened to the thud of his heart. Wearily he thought about courage, that there is nothing glorious or heroic about courage, that it has to do with thunderous pounding of the heart and sweat and terror and the humiliation of the self by compelling forces that drive one back against the wall, leaving one there, exposed, utterly alone.

It seemed a never-ending time until, at last, he slept. He slept. He was in a room full of office furniture, other people were standing about, sirens sounded, an air raid started, they all lay down on the floor. He crawled under a desk. When the bombs stopped falling, a telephone began to ring. Still lying on the floor, he reached up and held it to his ear. He heard children's voices which he recognized as the voices of his sons when they were little. Someone was playing a tape recording of one of their birthday parties into the phone. He smiled, delighted to hear the high piping voices, the laughter, the excitement. He waited for the tape to end, assuming that Margot would then talk to him, explain everything. The tape

128

ended. There was silence. He shouted—hullo hullo hullo into the phone, but there was no one at the other end. The phone was dead. Feeling afraid, he put down the phone and went to the window to see the bomb damage.

Through the window he could see the sun blazing over the garden. On the lawn there were three figures: a man tall and lean with thick bright hair was playing with a small boy, while a woman, buxom, motherly, in a red cotton sleveless dress and an orange straw hat with a floppy brim, was pruning a rosebush with secateurs that glinted in the sun. He banged on the window to get their attention but they ignored him. He struggled to open the window but it was stuck fast. He shouted, frantic for them to turn, to acknowledge him. The woman calmly snipped away at the green twigs, the man picked up the child, threw him up in the air and caught him. He could hear the child's laughter, but though he rattled the window, banged and shouted, he could not reach them. He felt a sharp pain in his chest. He placed his hand on his heart, felt something flat and hard under his palm, and struggled awake with the knowledge of the letter confronting him with the terror of its responsibility.

He got up and went to the window. The gray transparence of dawn thinly suffused the sky. Some birds were twittering. He took the folded page from his pocket and looked at it, submitting at last to what he had known squarely and with certainty beneath and beyond the stress and despair of his conflict. That only one choice was available to him. In that split second of recognition when Benedict had taken off his cap and revealed himself, he had recognized in the same breath that a responsibility would be placed upon him that he had no option but to discharge.

Wearily, he crossed the room, his shoulders sagging with the weight of his concession to the inevitable. At the bureau he stood for a long time considering bizarre methods of concealing the smuggled document. The wooden mask stared up at him from empty eyes, its primal simplicity asserting itself now as an archetypal symbol of dark warnings and omens of foreboding.

Giving himself up now to whatever forces for good or

evil would claim him, he folded the letter into a small square, pressing and flattening it to reduce its bulk, and slipped it into his leather billfold between his bank credit card and an invoice from Harrods for three cambric shirts.

When Rosie came in with the morning tea she found him sorting his things for packing. She said, "Up already, Paulie?" and set the tray down on the bedside table. A chased silver tray with an embroidered linen tray cloth, a delicate porcelain early-morning tea set that he remembered his mother taking tea from as she sat in bed surrounded by letters, magazines, and newspapers.

From the doorway Rosie said, "I've wrapped up the painting of Miss Margot for you, Paulie. I made a good strong parcel with a lot of cardboard and thick brown paper. Auw," she shook her head, sighed, "the study already looks different, empty without it." Abruptly, she left the room.

He sat down on the bed, poured the steaming amber brew into the cup and drank thirstily without bothering to add sugar or milk.

20

He kept filling his cup and drinking until the teapot was empty. He stood up and was drawn to the window by the vividness of his dream, as if he would see the three tranquilly engaged figures still on the lawn. There was nothing but the freshness of the new summer day.

His neck and limbs felt sore and stiff, his head ached. He bathed, shaved, dressed. Rosie came in with his laundry washed and ironed, with boxes of homemade delicacies for the children which she instructed him to handle with care. He finished his packing, wrapping the ostrich egg in a sweater, padding it well.

He took his luggage downstairs. The house was sluiced with clear early morning sunlight. Some birds were arguing noisily in the loquat tree outside the dining room window. The gardner was weeding a flower bed, whistling a monotonous dirgelike chant.

Now, the darkness had solidified inside him. He registered everything with his eyes and ears; beyond that, all impressions hit against the inpenetrable black.

Rosie placed a large wedge of melon in front of him. He ate it, unaware of its taste, temperature, texture. She brought eggs, toast, marmalade, tea. He consumed it all obediently. He knew all the motions he must go through, but they had no meaning further than their own execution.

He went up the stairs to his father's room. He could feel each leg on the tread of each stair as a lever bearing his weight upward.

He knocked on his father's door. Nurse opened it. She said, "Good morning, Doctor. Father is all spry and waiting for you," and went out as he came in.

His father was sitting up in bed, freshly bathed and shaved, his thick hair neatly brushed. His face looked pinched, pale. It was as if all his vitality was drawn into the shining mass of bright hair that flourished on his head.

He sat down on the bed.

"All packed, Paul?"

He nodded.

"Have you got the painting of Margot?"

"Rosie wrapped it beautifully, it's down in the hall with my luggage."

"Rosie told me she was baking some goodies for you to take to the boys."

"I've got them—all packed."

Downstairs the doorbell rang. They heard voices in the hall, Barney's stentorian, Una's mellifluous, Rosie's subdued.

"Barney and Una are taking you to the airport?"

He nodded.

"Paul." His father took his hand. "It's very good that you were able to come. It makes it all—a little easier for me now." He spoke slowly, pausing between sentences. "I feel quite—composed. Now—I don't want you to worry about me, I am going to manage quite well. If you hadn't come, I daresay it would have been hard on me. But your visit has given me—a reserve of quietness, and I feel—easier. Easier. It seems to me that this week we have had together has given us a chance—a chance to get close, that we might otherwise never have had. It's a rare thing, Paul, and we can consider ourselves fortunate. Now. Now—you must go back to your wife and your own sons, who need you, and you must get on with your life. Give them my very fond love. Take care of them—and take care of yourself too. And Paul, thank you."

He moved his weight forward and embraced his father. The bed seemed to be heaving and there were dry grating sounds. He was racked by his own huge dry painful sobbing. His father, very still, held him by his shoulders.

His blackness was a hollow, an emptiness that could never be filled. He had not cried since he was a boy. Now for a few minutes, clasping his father, his body wept of its own necessity. Briefly, the image of his dream appeared behind his eyelids, the man, the woman, the boy, engaged in the summer day.

He stood up, blew his nose, said, "I'm sorry, Dad."

"Don't be sorry, Paul. A man should know how to cry." His father looked calm. Below the crest of silver hair his face was drawn and gray.

They shook hands, not saying good-bye.

He went out, closed the door. He stood with his hand locked on the door handle, unable to find the will to break the contact. It seemed he would stand there immobile, indefinitely, incapable of taking the next step. He heard Nurse's creaking uniform coming along the passage. He turned.

She whispered, "I'll go and sit with him. Don't you worry now, and have a good trip home, Doctor dear." She let herself into the room.

He went downstairs. Una and Barney were in the dining room drinking coffee. The air was thick with the smell of smoke from Barney's cigar. Barney said, "We haven't got too much time, old man. We'll just finish our coffee and go and put your things in the car. We'll wait for you outside."

In the kitchen Rosie was scrubbing the wooden table with soap and a bristle brush. Here, over the years, she had kneaded the dough, rolled the pastry, mixed batters, chopped vegetables, pared fruits. Here he had done his homework, sat with his paint box and crayons and scissors and games when his parents were out and he alone in the house with Rosie. Over the years she had scoured the table with such vigor that the grain and whorls and knots in the wood surface stood whitely exposed.

She put down her brush, wiped her hands dry on her apron.

"Going now, Paulie?"

He nodded.

"You packed all that shortbread and fruitcake carefully?"

"Very carefully."

She sighed, shook her head. "Auw—the house will be empty without you."

He said, "Rosie, you know, when my father dies, you won't have to worry about yourself. He has taken care of you. There will be enough for you to live on."

"Yes, I know that. The old master is a good man. He has told me long ago that he has provided for me."

"What will you do?"

"I will go and live with Solly and his wife. I will help them with the children."

He thought, here is another one I am abandoning; *I* should be taking care of her in her old age, not poor Solly with his clubfeet. He said, "I believe there will be money for Solly too."

"Auw." She shook her head. "He is truly a good old gentleman, your father. Tell me, why is it, Master Paul, that good people like your father do not rule this country instead of those devils?"

He smiled at her. "It's a question that a lot of people have asked, Rosie, and no one knows the answer. But it seems—that kind gentle human beings are never really interested in—governing others. It's a pity."

"It really is." She sighed again. "Auw, you shouldn't leave yet, Paulie. You should wait till the old master goes."

"I can't stay any longer, Rosie."

"You will come back for the funeral?"

He shook his head.

"Auw!" She was angry. "Why can't you come back? They can't stop you, for your own father's funeral."

The kitchen clock ticked loudly on the Welsh dresser that was stacked with blue-and-white striped Cornish ware crockery.

"It's not right, Paulie. It's an unfinished business, this. A son must be with his father when he is dying, to help him into the next world. He must be there to cry by his father's grave. It's not right to go to your grave without your son to mourn beside you."

He understood now. Rosie was explaining to him why he had wept in his father's room. His tears were not about his dying. Not about the fear. They were about having to leave him to die. Some deep human order was being subverted by the unnaturalness of their forced separation. An ancient rhythm was being violated by aborted grief. Rosie understood this and was outraged. He understood now that some damage was being done for which no recompense, no consolation, was available.

Rosie was crying, "Don't go, Paulie, maybe it will be just a few more days to wait. Stay."

"I can't, Rosie, I'm not allowed to."

He put his arms around his old black mother. They stood together in the kitchen that had been her domain for nearly half a century. At the windows, the yellow curtains moved in a small breeze. The sunlight poured in, unconcerned, splashing over the red tiled floor.

She said, "Oh they are a bad lot. I'm telling you, Paulie, one day God will punish them. He will come down to punish them and set us all free."

He thought, oh Rosie, if God came down here, they would detain him indefinitely without accusation or trial or habeus corpus.

Outside Barney sounded the hooter.

Many times he had wept on Rosie's bosom. Now she wept on his.

Barney hooted again.

He squeezed her shoulders, turned, and left without saying good-bye.

Through the dining room, across the sitting room, out the french doors, across the terrace, down the broad stone steps onto the driveway. He got into the car and they drove away from the empty sunlit garden.

21

The car reeked of cigar smoke. They drove to the airport in silence. Once Barney spoke. He said, "There's that bastard behind us, following us to make sure you're leaving."

The lash of fear whipped at him. He thought, even my grief is defiled by them, contaminated by fear. His heart slowed at the thought of the flimsy bit of paper scarcely concealed in his wallet. He thought, there is danger only if Benedict is an agent of the Special Branch; otherwise it is unlikely that they will search me. They would be pleased to see him go, pleased to see the last of him. They use the Exit Permit to flush the country of undesirables—they had been reluctant to allow him to enter, they would want him promptly gone the moment his visa expired. Looking at his watch he saw there was an hour and three quarters more to run yet.

Through the car windows he noticed, dully, the sunlight abundant on trees, lawns, gardens. Another perfect day. No one ever noticed the weather here, it was wasted on them when every day dawned perfect and could not be contrasted with the austere beauty of winter, the frailty of spring, the melancholy of autumn. He wondered if it was raining in London, softly raining on Margot and the boys, steadily falling on the gray stone house in Hampstead. He watched a young man and woman, suntanned, dressed in brief white tennis togs, walking briskly swinging their rackets. He thought, there is a terrible price to pay for this beautiful climate.

He remembered *top* flat, *twen*ty-two, *chelt*enham gardens *lon*don, and looked out of the rearview window for his watcher. He could see the black Morris Minor two cars back, bowling along in the busy Saturday morning traffic. Caught between his compelling urgency to be with his family and his apprehension that they might prevent him, his being felt blank, suspended in a limbo of insubstantiality.

They were approaching the airport. The skin around his eyes and cheekbones felt dry and taut, and he remembered, numb now, the not-to-be-borne anguish that had assailed him at his father's bedside. He thought, this is something more harsh than grief, more shocking, like amputation.

Sitting hunched over his wretchedness alone on the back seat, Barney and Una grim and wordless in front, he thought about his father, thought how desolate and fearful it must feel, lying alone in his sun-filled bedroom waiting for the end to come, with no structured beliefs to support him as his hours dwindled; how his calmness in the presence of death was assumed, was a courageous charade to sustain his son through his own ordeal. Only saints don't dread death's final affirmation of our aloneness, our finiteness, he thought. Father is a good man, but he is no saint—saints don't enjoy a round of golf or a fine cognac after a well-cooked meal; saints don't have love affairs. And yet, he thought, as a jet roared low out of the cloudless blue of the sky, he is experienced with death—it's no stranger to him, he has had to deal with it again and again in his long career as a general practitioner. Perhaps then it's not such an alien fearful business to him.

But he would never know. The time had run out. It was too late now.

138

They were at the airport. The small black Morris parked quite openly behind them. The driver did not get out.

Barney and Una accompanied him through the lounges and corridors as far as they could go. He was anxious to leave them, to relieve them of his uncleanness, this outcast they had on their hands who spread unnatural grief and tears upon those who loved him.

He shook hands with Barney, could not speak, could not thank him. Una held him, tears raining down her kind cheeks, dampening his face.

For the third time in one morning, he had to will himself to turn and walk away.

At the exit barrier an elderly official took his passport, studied his visa, regarded him curiously and took up a large ledgerlike volume from beneath the counter. Licking his forefinger he proceeded, unhurriedly, to turn page after page of what appeared to be printed lists. Slowly he ran his finger down a column, paused, peering myopically at the fine print for a minute that seemed to take an eternity to pass through three hundred and sixty degrees on the indifferent face of the clock behind him. Without looking up he closed the book, removed the currency form, and handed back the passport.

He waited, will-less. Waited for the order, the barked instruction, the grasp on his shoulder.

Awed then, overwhelmed by the weight of the responsibility of the freedom to choose, he moved tentatively away from the desk. Afraid to turn around, he walked, hurried, listening for footsteps behind him, listening to the noise of his heart. His mouth dry, palms clammy, he walked quickly toward the exit gate. Down a corridor, through an open door out onto the blazing tarmac. No one stopped him. There was the VC10 waiting. He showed his boarding pass, climbed the stairway. A cool English air hostess showed him to his seat by the window. He sat down, buckled his seat belt. He was tense, coiled up like a spring. He started visibly when a woman and child arrived to occupy the two seats beside him.

He stared out of the window at the flat airport buildings with the sun glaring down on them, thought of London airport shrouded in chilling rain.

The throbbing of engines abraded him. His nails bit into his palms as the plane taxied along the runway.

Growing right up alongside the runway, he could see tall sere grass blowing lazily, indifferent to the encroachment of concrete, the oil splashes, the violent discord of the screaming jet engines. Through the grass, the dry red earth of Africa could be seen, sunbaked, enduring, continuing right under the layer of concrete that had been thinly plastered upon its ancient surface.

He saw the grassy veld falling away beneath him. The hold on his being unclenched tentatively. As the plane rose, he felt his heart rising with it.